50 GREAT Stories

FOR 7 TO 9 YEAR-OLDS

First published in 2001 by Miles Kelly Publishing,
Bardfield Centre, Great Bardfield, Essex CM7 4SL
info@mileskelly.net

Printed in China

Project manager: Paula Borton
Editorial Assistant: Isla MacCuish

British Library Cataloguing-in-Publication Data
A catalogue record for this book is available from the British Library

ISBN 1-84236-015-9

24681097531

Cover artwork by Pam Smy

Visit us on the web:
www.mileskelly.net

Acknowledgements

The Cloth of Dreams THE BOY AND THE CLOTH OF DREAMS text © 1994 Jenny Koralek. Illustrations © 1994 James Mayhew. Reproduced by permission of the publisher Walker Books Ltd., London. *The Girl Who Couldn't Walk* From Tales of Wonder and Magic by Berlie Doherty published courtesy of Walker Books Ltd. *The Giant Who Threw Tantrums* David L Harrison for permission to reprint from The Book of Giant Stories, 1972, co-published by Jonathan Cape, Ltd (England) and American Heritage Press (USA). *A New Arrival* From Ms Wiz Spells Trouble by Terence Blacker reproduced courtesy of Macmillan Children's Books, London. *The King With Dirty Feet, The Big Wide-Mouthed Toad-Frog* The King With Dirty Feet © Pomme Clayton 1991. The Big-Wide-Mouthed Toad-Frog © Patrick Ryan 1991, both from TIME FOR TELLING: A COLLECTION OF STORIES FROM AROUND THE WORLD Selected by Mary Medlicott. Reproduced by permission of Kingfisher Publications plc. All rights reserved. *Monster Film* Monster Film by Russell Hoban reproduced by permission of Hodder and Stoughton Limited. All other stories written by Vic Parker. The publishers have made every effort to contact all copyright holders, but apologise if any source remains unacknowledged.

50 GREAT Stories

FOR 7 TO 9 YEAR-OLDS

EDITED BY VIC PARKER

Miles KeLLy
PUBLISHING

Contents

SPELLS AND ENCHANTMENT

The Pot of Gold *Illustrated by Sally Holmes*   9

The Wild Swans *Illustrated by Tricia Newell*   12

The Pied Piper of Hamelin *Illustrated by Sally Holmes*   19

Belle and the Beast *Illustrated by Cecilia Johansson*   23

Pandora's Box *Illustrated by Caroline Sharpe*   30

Tomlin *Illustrated by Vanessa Card*   34

Hop Toads and Pearls *Illustrated by Priscilla Lamont*   38

The Firebird *Illustrated by Pam Smy*   42

The Red Shoes *Illustrated by Peter Utton*   49

The Magic Tinderbox *Illustrated by Sally Holmes*   53

The Cloth of Dreams *Illustrated by James Mayhew*   60

Contents

FAVOURITES

Seven At One Blow *Illustrated by Tracy Morgan*   64

Ali Baba and the Forty Thieves *Illustrated by Rachel Merriman*   68

The Little Matchgirl *Illustrated by Sally Holmes*   75

St Christopher *Illustrated by Mike White*   78

Thumbelina *Illustrated by Julie Banyard*   81

Babushka *Illustrated by Mike White*   86

Rip Van Winkle *Illustrated by Susan Scott*   91

The Girl Who Couldn't Walk *Illustrated by Pam Smy*   96

A Tall Story *Illustrated by Peter Utton*   104

The Adventures of Sinbad the Sailor *Illustrated by Susan Scott*   106

The Old Woman and her Pig *Illustrated by Priscilla Lamont*   110

The Brave Tin Soldier *Illustrated by Susan Scott*   113

Contents

FEATHER, FUR AND FANGS

Puss in Boots *Illustrated by Julie Banyard* 117

The Wonderful Tar Baby *Illustrated by Caroline Sharpe* 122

The Big-Wide-Mouthed Toad-Frog *Illustrated by Sally Holmes* 125

The Dragons of Peking *Illustrated by Rachel Merriman* 131

The Hare and the Tortoise *Illustrated by Priscilla Lamont* 136

Monster Film *Illustrated by Ross Collins* 139

The Elephant's Child *Illustrated by Rachel Merriman* 149

The Moon in the Pond *Illustrated by Caroline Sharpe* 152

The Last of the Dragons *Illustrated by Susan Scott* 157

GIANTS, WITCHES AND GENIES

The Giant Who Threw Tantrums *Illustrated by Tracy Morgan* 167

Baba Yaga, The Bony Legged *Illustrated by Julie Banyard* 171

The Selfish Giant *Illustrated by Peter Utton* 176

Aladdin and the Lamp *Illustrated by Pam Smy* 180

In the Castle of Giant Cruelty *Illustrated by Vanessa Card* 188

A New Arrival *Illustrated by Cecilia Johansson* 192

Contents

David and the Giant *Illustrated by Mike White*   197

The Fisherman and the Bottle *Illustrated by Susan Scott*   201

The Giant's Wife *Illustrated by Sally Holmes*   205

The Thunder God Gets Married *Illustrated by Tracy Morgan*   210

ROYAL ADVENTURES

The King With Dirty Feet *Illustrated by Rachel Merriman*   214

The Emperor's New Clothes *Illustrated by Priscilla Lamont*   220

The Little Mermaid *Illustrated by Tracy Morgan*   226

The Golden Touch *Illustrated by Vanessa Card*   233

The Nutcracker Prince *Illustrated by Julie Banyard*   236

The Sword in the Stone *Illustrated by Sally Holmes*   241

Ricky with the Tuft *Illustrated by Cecilia Johansson*   245

The Happy Prince *Illustrated by Pam Smy*   251

Spells and Enchantment

THE POT OF GOLD

an Irish folk tale

Niall O'Leary was sitting on a gate in the sunshine, day-dreaming quite happily, when – TIC! TIC! TIC! – he became aware of a sharp sound coming from the field behind him.

"Now what on earth can that be?" Niall wondered to himself. "It's too loud to be a grasshopper . . . and it's too quiet to be a bird."

TIC! TIC! TIC! it went.

Niall O'Leary swung his legs over the gate and turned around. He blinked in astonishment. There in the long grass of the field was the tiniest man Niall had ever seen, no higher than his boot. The tiny man had his back to Niall, but Niall could see that he was dressed all in green, with a long white feather in his cap. A tiny leather shoe lay before him on a rock, and he was banging away at it with a tiny stone hammer.

Niall's eyes lit up. A leprechaun! A real, live leprechaun! Niall licked his lips greedily.

Every tiny leprechaun had a huge pot of gold hidden somewhere. And as everybody knew, if you caught hold of a leprechaun and squeezed him tightly enough, he would have to tell you where his treasure was buried.

Quietly, quietly, Niall O'Leary got down from the gate.

TIC! TIC! TIC! went the leprechaun's hammer.

Quietly, quietly, Niall O'Leary crept through the grass.

TIC! TIC! TIC! went the leprechaun's hammer.

Quietly, quietly, Niall O'Leary reached out with his large, meaty hands . . .

"GOTCHA!" cried Niall O'Leary, and he squeezed and squeezed the wriggling leprechaun with all his might.

"Ooooof!" cried the leprechaun. "Let me go, you big bully!"

"Tell me where your gold is and I will!" boomed Niall.

"I can't tell you anything while you're squeezing the breath out of me," the leprechaun gasped, looking rather purple.

"Oops, sorry!" blustered Niall, and he relaxed his grip a little.

"That's better," wheezed the leprechaun, taking big gulps of air. "Now put me down and I promise I'll show you where my gold is hidden."

A broad grin spread across Niall's face as he lowered the leprechaun back down to the grass. "A leprechaun can't break his promise!" he chuckled.

"No," grumbled the leprechaun rather crossly, "and my gold is buried under here." He leapt a few steps into the middle of the field and pointed at a clump of dandelions. "You'll need a spade, mind," the leprechaun added thoughtfully. "You'll have to dig quite a way down."

Niall's face fell. "But I haven't got a spade with me," he said, glumly. "What shall I do?"

"Why don't you tie your handkerchief around the dandelions so you don't forget where the gold is buried," the leprechaun suggested. "Then hurry back home and fetch a spade. I promise on my word of honour that I won't untie the handkerchief."

Niall's face brightened once again. "What a great idea!" he beamed. He fumbled in his pocket, brought out a rather grubby red silk handkerchief, and tied it around the clump of dandelions. It waved at him in the breeze like a cheerful flag. "Thank you Mr Leprechaun," Niall remembered to say politely. "You've been mighty helpful." Then in a few strides, he was back over the gate and away home, humming merrily.

As soon as Niall had grabbed the biggest spade he could find in the garden shed, he set off back to the field at once. All the way down the lane, he day-dreamed of what he would do with the gold. But when Niall O'Leary reached the gate, he stopped stone-still and his mouth hung open. He dropped the spade and scratched his head. "Well, blow me down," gasped Niall. All over the field, thousands of red silk handkerchiefs were tied onto clumps of dandelions and fluttering in the breeze. And Niall could hear the sound of gleeful leprechaun laughter floating over the grass on the wind.

So Niall O'Leary never got his pot of gold after all. But that is how he came to own the most successful silk handkerchief shop in the whole of Ireland . . .

THE WILD SWANS

a retelling from the original story by Hans Christian Andersen

A long time ago, in a land far away, there lived a king whose wife died, leaving him with eleven little sons and a baby daughter, Elise. The king married again and the children's new stepmother was cruel and jealous. She seemed to put the king under a wicked spell which made him forget all about his beloved children. So the queen sent little Elise away from the palace to be brought up by a peasant couple who lived in the forest. Then she used witchcraft to turn the princes into swans and she sent them flying off from the palace forever.

Many years passed and Elise thought she would never see her brothers again. Then one evening, as she was sitting by a lake watching the sun set, she saw a line of swans come flying like a white ribbon across the sky. They alighted next to her, and at the exact moment when the sun melted into the lake, the swans disappeared in a flutter of feathers. In their place stood eleven princes. They were Elise's long-lost brothers! They recognised each other at once, and they ran to hug each other, weeping tears of joy.

"We have to live as swans by day," the princes explained, "but at night we return to our true selves. Our wicked stepmother banished us to live in a country which lies across a wide sea and we are only allowed to return here once a year for just eleven days. Tomorrow is the day that we must leave once again. Little sister, it is a dangerous journey, but now we have found you, we will take you with us."

All night long, the princes gathered willow bark and tough reeds and rushes and Elise wove them into a strong net. By sunrise, as the princes fluttered back into swans, Elise was lying in the woven mesh, fast asleep. The swans seized the net strings and, with a few powerful wingbeats, sped off into the sky. And so the brothers carried their sister, right across the land and over the churning sea . . .

High above the waves, Elise dreamed she saw a beautiful fairy who smiled sadly and said, "If you are very brave, you can set your brothers free from their enchantment. You must go to the churchyard and pick the stinging nettles that grow on the graves there. They will burn and blister your skin, but you must pick them with your bare hands and then crush them with your bare feet. Twine the nettles

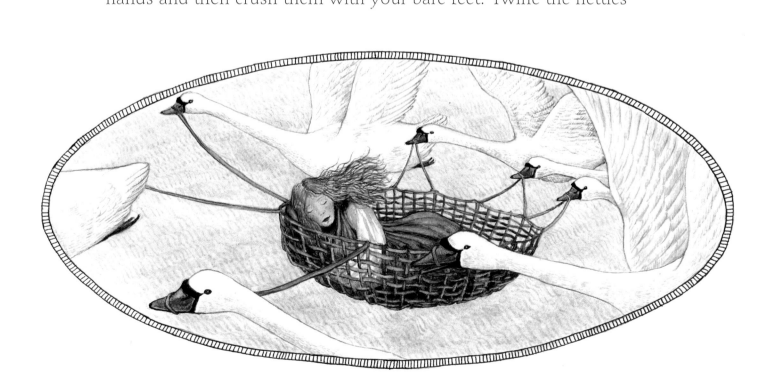

into flax and weave eleven shirts with long sleeves. The second that you throw the shirts over your brothers, they will be swans no longer. But mark this well, from the moment you start your task, you must not speak. If you utter a single word, it will be like a dagger through your brothers' hearts and they will surely die."

Elise awoke with a start to find herself lying on a bed of moss in a great cavern, shaded with vines and creepers. Her brothers were flown, and strangely there was a stinging nettle lying next to her. At once, she slipped away to find the churchyard. The graves were silent and spooky, but Elise clambered all over them collecting the nettles that sprang there in thick clumps. How the nettles burnt and blistered her hands! Elise hurried back to the cave and trampled on the nettles until they were crushed and her feet swollen and sore. Finally, she twisted the stalks into flax and began carefully to weave . . .

Elise's work was clumsy and slow due to her red, painful hands and arms. But by the evening when the swans returned, she had woven nearly half of the first shirt. The princes were upset by Elise's strange task and scared by her silence. But when they saw the spark of hope in Elise's eyes, they realised that she must be suffering for their sake. The youngest brother wept for his sister's pain, and as his tears fell onto her injured arms and hands, the blisters healed themselves and disappeared.

Elise would have worked around the clock, until all eleven shirts were finished and the spell finally broken. However, the next day, her hiding place in the cavern was sniffed out by hunting dogs and a royal hunting party burst in upon her. Elise was terrified, but she knew that if she uttered a single word, her brothers would die. The king thought that Elise was the most beautiful girl he had ever seen. "Don't be afraid," he said gently to her, as she stood trembling and silent. "Whoever you are, you can't live here in this cave. You will come back to my palace and I will make sure you are looked after and taken care of." The king lifted Elise up behind him

on his horse and they were off like the wind over the hills.

Elise wept without a word as the ladies of the court dressed her in silks and satins, threaded pearls in her hair, and led her into a splendid banquet which the king had ordered in her honour. "You will be my queen," the king told Elise gently after the feast, "but I do not want you to be sad. I want you to be happy here with me." The king led Elise down a corridor to a small door. He opened it and Elise's mouth widened into a perfect "O" of surprise. The room was adorned with green hangings, to look just like the cave in the forest. And on the floor was the shirt she had finished and all the bundles of nettles from the churchyard. Elise flung her arms around the king and kissed his face and hands as he handed her the key to the little room.

After that, Elise spent every day at the king's side. She could see that he was good and kind and thoughtful, and she longed to tell him how much she had begun to care for him – but she dared not utter a sound. Every night, Elise crept down the corridor in her nightdress to her secret little room and continued with her weaving. Her heart was heavy with the thought that her brothers did not know where she was and must be searching anxiously for her.

Night after night, the pile of flax grew lower and lower, and by the time the tenth shirt was finished, Elise was in desperate need of more nettles. There was nothing for it but to creep out of the palace by moonlight, and hurry down the dark paths all the way to the churchyard. When Elise reached the graves, her blood ran cold with horror. Witches sat on the tombstones, reaching down into the earth with their bony fingers. Elise thought of her brothers and forced herself to walk past the witches and collect huge armfuls of the burning nettles. Then she was away, hurrying back to the palace before dawn . . .

Unbeknown to Elise, the king's chief advisor had spied on her. He had always been jealous of the wild, silent girl from the cave who had won the king's heart and now sat at the king's side instead of him. His wicked heart leapt for joy as he hurried to the king the very next morning. "Your majesty," the chief advisor whispered, "I am sorry to tell you that I saw your bride-to-be at the churchyard last night, surrounded by witches. She can only have been performing black magic."

The king shook his head vigorously. "You must be mistaken," he said. "I do not believe it."

"Go to Elise's room and see the new pile of churchyard nettles she collected for her spells," the chief advisor insisted. "She is a witch and she must be burnt. The people will find out and they will demand it."

The king hung his head in sorrow. He felt as though his heart was breaking.

Next morning, guards broke into Elise's chamber and hauled her away to a dark, damp prison. They left her with only her nettles for a pillow and the shirts she had woven to keep her warm but they were all Elise wanted. Elise didn't know what she had done wrong, but she knew she was going to die and that she didn't have much time left. Her hands trembled as she hurried desperately to finish the final shirt. As she twisted and plaited and wove, a swan came flapping his wings against the window. Elise recognised her youngest brother and she ran to thrust her fingers through the bars and stroke his feathers. She couldn't say a word to tell him what had happened, and tears sparkled in her eyes as she waved him away and hurried back to her work . . .

All day and all night, Elise's sore fingers worked faster than ever. As the sun's rays stretched through the bars, the final shirt was nearly, nearly finished . . . Elise didn't stop frantically working even when the guards thrust her into a smelly cart and they went bumping through the streets. Crowds of people threw mud at her and jeered. "Look at the witch!" they shouted. "See, she's working on some evil spell!"

Then the cart arrived at the bonfire and the executioner stepped forwards to drag Elise to her death. But suddenly, eleven huge white swans swooped down out of the sky. Quick as a flash, Elise grabbed the shirts and threw them over the birds.

The crowd fell back in terror as there was a huge flash of lightning. The swans disappeared and in their places stood eleven handsome princes – although the youngest had a swan's wing instead of one arm, for Elise had run out of time to finish the final sleeve of his shirt.

"Now I can speak!" Elise sobbed. "I am innocent!" She sank into her brothers' arms and the princes explained all that had happened. Then the people began to cheer and the church bells rang out for joy, and the king took his beautiful bride and her brothers back home to his palace.

THE PIED PIPER OF HAMELIN
a German legend

Imagine what it would be like to live in a town overrun by rats. Rats in the streets, the shops, the gardens! Rats in the town hall, the hospital and police station! Rats in your school corridors, your classroom, your desk! Rats in your kitchen, your bath, your bed! Well, that's what it was like to live in the town of Hamelin, which lay beside the River Weser.

No one knew where the rats had come from or how they had managed to take over the town in such numbers. The townspeople of Hamelin were desperate to be rid of them. They couldn't eat without rats nibbling off their plates. They couldn't get dressed without uncovering rats nesting in their clothes and boots. They couldn't put their babies down to sleep without finding rats cuddled up in the cradles. They couldn't even chat to each other in comfort, for the noise of all the squeaking and scampering! So you can see why the mayor put up a poster outside the town hall saying:

There will be a reward of
ONE THOUSAND GUILDERS
to anyone who can get rid of the rats!

Yes, one thousand guilders! Everyone began to imagine what they would do with such a huge fortune – but of course, they could only dream. No one had the first idea how to begin claiming their town back from the rats.

By the time the stranger came knocking on the door of the town hall, the mayor was panic-stricken. He would have listened to anybody who said they could help. So when the stranger announced confidently, "I can get rid of all the rats for you," the mayor didn't worry too much about the stranger's odd, multicoloured costume. The mayor paid no attention to the stranger's extraordinarily long fingers and the unusual pipe that hung on a cord round his neck. The mayor didn't think too much about the sad smile on the stranger's face or the wistful gleam in his eyes. The mayor just beamed with relief and said, "GREAT! When can you begin?"

"Right now," replied the stranger, and he raised his pipe to his lips. Off he went, out of the town hall and into the street, playing a lilting tune that filled the air. Instantly, all over town, the rats stopped scuffling, pricked up their ears, and listened. For the first time in many, many months, there was silence for a moment. Then the scampering and squeaking began again, as the rats ran to follow the Pied Piper.

The townspeople of Weser couldn't believe their eyes. All through the town strolled the Pied Piper, his fingers continually moving on his pipe and the haunting notes rippling through the air. And out of all the houses swarmed the rats; out of every garden and gutter, out of every nook and cranny they came streaming. Down stairwells and through streets, out of passages and alleyways, over rooftops and along roads the rats came hurrying after the strange musician. And the Pied Piper didn't stop playing all the way to the wide River Weser. He didn't stop playing as he dipped one brightly coloured foot into the rushing waters and the thousands of rats began to plunge off the bank into the river. He didn't stop playing until the very last rat had drowned.

Then the church bells rang out in celebration, the townspeople started hugging each other, the children began dancing and singing – and the Pied Piper strode quietly back to the town hall to fetch his reward.

"My one thousand guilders, if you please," said the Pied Piper, calmly.

The mayor just smiled what he thought was a charming smile. Now the rats were dead and gone he certainly didn't plan on giving away what was nearly the entire contents of the town council bank account! "Come, come now, my dear fellow," the mayor coaxed. "One thousand guilders is somewhat over-the-top for playing a pretty ditty on a tin whistle, surely you'll agree! Why don't we settle on fifty guilders, and I'll throw in a nice bronze medal and even put up a statue of you and me together in the market place, eh?"

The Pied Piper simply turned on his heel and walked out into the street.

As he went, he once more lifted his pipe to his lips. But this time, he played a different tune. Enchanting notes rippled all around and down the roads the children came dancing, running and leaping after the Pied Piper.

The men and women of Hamelin were struck still with horror as the children swept past them and were gone through the town. Playing his strange melody, the Pied Piper led the children past the River Weser and skipping happily along a path that led up to a steep, craggy mountain. He piped a burst of airy notes and a little door appeared in the mountain slope. The Pied Piper led the children inside. The townspeople could hear the echo of his pipe and the children's laughter grow fainter and fainter as they went deeper and deeper into the earth. Then suddenly, the little door slammed shut and disappeared. The children were gone – all except for one little boy who was lame and so hadn't been able to keep up with the others. He stood on the mountainside and sobbed, calling out for his friends. But the little door had vanished.

No one ever saw the Pied Piper or the children again. But on sunny days, some townsfolk swore they could hear ripples of childish laughter floating down from the mountain. And from that day to this, there has never been a single rat in the town of Hamelin.

BELLE AND THE BEAST

a retelling from the original tale by Madame Leprince de Beaumont

here was once a businessman who had made a fortune by trading overseas. He lived in a magnificent mansion staffed by servants and with a TV in every room – including the indoor swimming pool. The businessman's wife had died, so he had brought up their three beautiful daughters on his own. Unfortunately, the two eldest girls, Bianca and Bettina, lazed about all day watching chat shows, flicking through magazines and day-dreaming of marrying professional footballers. But Belle, the youngest daughter, was a great help to her father in running his business. She also enjoyed reading books on engineering and space exploration, for she was as intelligent as she was beautiful, and she had an avid interest in rocket science.

The businessman once had to go away on an important trip for work.

"Don't forget to bring us back some jewellery!" yelled Bianca.

"And some perfume!" bellowed Bettina.

"Is there nothing you would like, darling?" the businessman asked Belle.

Belle thought for a while. "Just a beautiful rose, please Daddy," she smiled.

"That's my girl!" the businessman said, and gave a cheery wave as he drove away.

But when the businessman finally returned, he was downcast and empty-handed.

"I'm afraid your dear old Dad has had it," the businessman explained. "I was on my way back last night, but it was dark and raining and somehow I got completely lost in the middle of nowhere. The only house for miles around was a spooky old mansion, and I went to ask for help. The lights were on, the front door was open, but nobody seemed to be at home. I thought it was very strange, but I was so desperate that I crept inside and stayed the night. Early this morning, as I was hurrying off through the grounds, I stopped to pick a rose for Belle. 'STOP THIEF!' someone roared. 'This is my house and those are my roses! Is this how you repay my hospitality? I am going to kill you!' The man who came striding towards me was uglier than a monster in a film. He had a hairy face and bloodshot eyes, a snout for a nose and teeth like fangs. His hands were clawed and his body huge and hulking. I realised that the beast was deadly serious, so I fell on my knees in terror and begged for mercy. 'I will give you three months to say goodbye to everyone,' he growled. 'After that, you must return here to die . . . unless you have a daughter who is willing to come in your place and live here with me forever.'"

Bianca and Bettina stood gawping in horror. "Oh Daddy," they wailed, "who is going to look after us when you're gone?"

"Don't worry, Daddy," Belle comforted her father. "I can't let you die. I will go instead of you."

"Belle, you will do nothing of the kind!" her father protested. "You haven't seen this guy!"

"I don't care!" said Belle, resolutely sticking out her chin. And nothing Belle's father could say would make her change her mind. "If you sneak off without me, I shall just follow you," was her final word on the subject. So three months later, the broken-hearted businessman accompanied his brave daughter to the door of the huge, lonely mansion and kissed her for the last time. He could hardly see through his tears as he turned and walked away . . .

"Right," Belle said to herself firmly, though her bottom lip was trembling. "Let's find the library. Maybe it has a good science section." She set off through the stone corridors and oak-panelled halls, exploring. It was an eerie feeling to be all alone in such an enormous old place. Suddenly, Belle stopped in surprise. There, right in front of her was a door marked 'Belle's room'. She put her hand on the iron handle and gently pushed. It swung open with a creak. Belle gasped with delight. Inside, was everything she could possibly have wished for. There was a soft, white bed. Wardrobes full of beautiful clothes. But best of all, lining the walls was shelf after shelf of books.

"The owner of this place can't be all bad," Belle murmured to herself. She drew down the nearest book. It was bound in ancient leather and had gold-edging. She read the first page:

Belle, you have a heart of gold
Like girls in fairytales of old.
Whatever you wish, it will come true
There's magic waiting here for you.

"Hmmm," wondered Belle. "Well, the only thing I really wish is that I could see if my Dad is okay."

At that very moment, Belle noticed a mirror on the bedroom wall begin to cloud over. Mists swirled across the glass, and when they cleared, instead of her own reflection, she saw a picture of her father, sitting at home sadly without her. After a few moments the picture vanished, but Belle was very grateful to have been able to see her father at all. *The owner of this place is actually very kind*, Belle thought to herself.

Just then, Belle heard the dinner bell ringing from the great hall. She hurried along and found a delicious meal laid out for one. No sooner had she swallowed three mouthfuls than she heard a shuffling and a snuffling. The food stuck in her throat and her heartbeat quickened. Belle forced herself to turn round and face her host.

Her father had been right. He was truly hideous.

"I'm Belle," she whispered, remembering her manners, like the well-brought up girl she was. "My room is wonderful – thank you."

"Call me Beast," said the monster gruffly, a look of pleasure lighting up his sad eyes. "Did you really like everything?"

"Yes, of course," said Belle. "Particularly the books. I love books, especially those on rocket science."

"They are your books now," said Beast. "Everything here is yours. I give it all to you. You can do with everything just what you wish. That goes for me, too. If I'm bothering you just tell me to go away and I will." The Beast looked down at his huge, flat feet. "I know I'm exceedingly ugly. I might put you off your food." He sighed a deep sigh. "And not only am I ugly, I'm very stupid too."

"Now, now," comforted Belle. "I'm sure that's not the case. Anyone who is ready to say they are stupid can't possibly be stupid. The only people who really are stupid are those who won't admit that they're stupid!"

"Do you really think so?" sighed the Beast.

"Yes, of course!" laughed Belle. "And if you're really worried about being stupid, I can teach you all about rocket science. Let me get my books . . ."

A sheepish smile came over the Beast's ugly face as he listened to Belle read. After a while, he suddenly interrupted her.

"Belle, will you marry me?" he asked.

Belle was extremely taken aback. She looked at the monster as he crouched adoringly in front of her. "I'm sorry," she said. "I wish I could, but I really don't want to."

And so the time passed. Each day, Belle read in her room and walked in the beautiful grounds, admiring the roses. And each evening, the Beast came to visit her. As the weeks went on, Belle began to enjoy his company and looked forward to seeing him. But each night the Beast asked her to marry him, and even though Belle liked him more and more as a friend, she simply couldn't – well, *fancy* him.

Belle's only other worry was her Dad. Each day she saw in the mirror that he was pining more and more without her. Her sisters were selfish, unkind and thoughtless, and her father had grown quiet and pale and thin.

"Dear Beast," Belle begged one night, "allow me to go back to see my dad. I am afraid that he is dying of a broken heart."

Much to Belle's surprise, the Beast nodded his agreement. "Of course, Belle," he said, "if that is what will make you happy. Only I don't know what I'll do without you . . ."

"Darling Beast," whispered Belle, stroking his matted, shaggy hair, "I promise I'll be back in a week."

"Then I promise you that when you wake up tomorrow morning, you'll be at home with your father," sighed the Beast. "Take this ring. When you're ready to leave, just put it by the side of your bed at night. As you sleep, it will bring you back here."

Sure enough, next morning Belle woke up back in her old bed. Her dad couldn't believe his eyes! He and Belle hugged and laughed and spent a wonderful holiday doing all the things they used to enjoy doing together – going through his accounts, visiting the science museum, watching old musicals on TV . . . The week flew by in the twinkling of an eye. "Please, Belle, don't go," begged her dad, and Belle didn't have the heart to leave.

But several nights later, Belle had a terrible dream. She saw the Beast lying in the garden of his mansion, under the rose bushes that he loved so much. Belle knew that he was dying. "Daddy," she sobbed the next morning. "I'm worried that something dreadful has happened to the Beast. He's my best and truest friend – and it's all my fault!"

That night, Belle put the Beast's ring by her bedside. It didn't seem as if she'd been asleep for five minutes when she woke up in her beautiful white room in the mansion. Belle sped off into the moonlit garden and there, lying under the rose bushes just as in her dream, lay the Beast. She flung herself down by his side and heaved his big, heavy head into her lap. Her tears plopped one by one onto his hairy face.

Weakly, the Beast opened his eyes and smiled. "I thought you had forgotten your promise," he whispered. "Now I have seen you once again, I can die happily."

"No!" Belle cried. "You can't die! You mustn't leave me! I love you!" And she kissed him.

At that very moment, the night sky was lit up by a million rainbow-coloured fireworks. Belle gazed upwards in surprise – she thought things like that only happened in films. When she looked back down at the Beast again, the monster was gone. Lying in her lap was a handsome, happy prince. He sprang up and lifted Belle to her feet with joy in his eyes.

"My darling Belle," he told her, "Thank you for setting me free! I have lived under a wicked enchantment for years which forced me to appear as the Beast – not only ugly but stupid, too – until a beautiful girl willingly fell in love with me. You are the only person in the world who saw through my ugly appearance and sensed what I was really like inside. Now we will live together happily forever."

And that's exactly what they did. But this is a real tale, not a fairytale, and real tales don't have entirely happy endings. The prince took Belle to live at his palace – and her dad went to live with them too. But Belle's selfish sisters got what they deserved. They were turned into statues and set at the palace gates until such time as they began to think about other people rather than themselves. As far as I know, they're both there still . . .

PANDORA'S BOX
a Greek myth

hen the world was first created, it was a happy place of light and laughter; there was no such thing as sadness or pain. The sun shone every day and the gods came down from heaven to walk and talk with the humans who lived on earth.

One afternoon, a man called Epimetheus and his wife, Pandora, were outside tending their flower garden when they saw the god Mercury approaching. He was bowed down by a dark wooden chest that he was carrying on his shoulders and he looked hot and tired. Pandora rushed to get the worn-out god a cool drink, while Epimetheus helped him lower the chest onto the ground. It was tied shut with golden cords and was carved with strange markings.

"My friends, would you do me a great favour?" sighed Mercury. "It is so hot today and the box is so heavy! May I leave it here while I go on an errand?"

"Of course you can," smiled Epimetheus.

The man and the god heaved the chest indoors.

"Are you sure that no one will find it?" asked Mercury

anxiously. "NO ONE under ANY circumstances must open the box."

"Don't worry," laughed Epimetheus and Pandora, and they waved the god off through the trees.

All of a sudden, Pandora stopped still and frowned. "Listen, Epimetheus!" she hissed. "I am sure I heard someone whispering our names!"

Epimetheus and Pandora listened hard. At first, they heard nothing but the twittering of the birds in the sunshine and the rustling of the leaves in the breeze. Then, they heard the distant sound of "Epimetheus! Pandora!" being called from outside.

"It's our friends!" cried Epimetheus, happily.

But Pandora looked puzzled and shook her head. "No, Epimetheus, those aren't the voices I heard," she said, firmly.

"They must have been!" Epimetheus laughed. "Come on now, let's go and see everyone."

"You go," Pandora insisted, with a frown. "I'd rather stay here for a while."

Epimetheus shrugged, kissed Pandora on the nose, and strode outside. As soon as he was gone,

Pandora hurried over to the strange box and waited. After only a few seconds, she heard it again – distant voices calling "Pandora! Pandora!" The voices were so low and whispery that Pandora wasn't sure whether she really was hearing them or was just imagining it.. She bent down closer and put her ear to the lid. No, this time she was sure. The box was calling to her! "Pandora!" the voices pleaded. "Let us out, Pandora! We are trapped in here in the darkness! Please help us to escape!"

Pandora jumped back with a start. Mercury had expressly forbade them or anyone else to open the box . . . and yet the voices sounded so sad and pitiful.

"Pandora!" they came again. "Help us! Help us, we beg you!"

Pandora could stand it no longer. Hurriedly, she knelt down and worked at the tight golden knots. All the time, the whispering and pleading voices filled her ears. At last the knots were undone and the gleaming cords fell away. She took a deep breath and opened the lid.

At once, Pandora realised she had done a terrible thing. The box had been crammed with all the evils in the world – thousands of tiny, brown, moth-like creatures that stung people with their wings and caused hurt and misery wherever they went. Now, thanks to Pandora, the evils were free! They flew up out of the chest in a great swarm and fluttered all over Pandora's skin. For the very first time, Pandora felt pain and regret. She began to wail with despair, and all too late, she slammed the lid back down onto the box.

Outside, Epimetheus heard his wife's cries and came running as fast as he could. The little creatures fluttered to sting and bite him, before speeding off through the window into the world beyond. For the first time ever, Epimetheus began to shout at his wife in anger. Pandora yelled back, and the couple realised in horror that they were arguing.

"Let me out!" interrupted a high voice. Pandora and Epimetheus grabbed onto each other in a panic. The voice was coming from inside the box. "Don't be afraid of me! Let me out and I can help you!" came the voice once more.

"What do you think?" Pandora whispered to Epimetheus, wide-eyed.

"Surely you can't do any more mischief than you already have done," he grumbled. So Pandora shut her eyes and opened Mercury's chest for a second time.

Out of the deep, dark box fluttered a single shining white spirit like a butterfly. It was Hope. Pandora and Epimetheus sobbed with relief as she fluttered against their skin and soothed their stinging wounds. Then she was gone, darting out of the window and into the world after the evils. And luckily, Hope has stayed with us ever since.

TOMLIN
a Scottish folk tale

Carterhaugh Wood was thick and green and dark, and people said it was the home of fairy folk. One bright summer's day, Janet, the earl's daughter, made up her mind to go and explore it for herself. She crept out of the castle and set off down a narrow path deep into the woods. After a while, Janet reached a small stone well in the middle of a clearing. There were roses climbing all over it – far more beautiful than any in the castle gardens – and Janet bent to pick one. No sooner had the stem broken off in her hand than Janet heard a voice that said, "Naughty-naughty, Janet. Who said you could come here into our wood and pick one of our roses?"

Janet straightened up with a start. There before her stood the most handsome young knight she had ever seen. She tossed her hair proudly and replied, "How dare you speak to me like that! These woods belong to my father, the earl. I shall go where I choose and pick whatever flowers I like!"

Delight sparkled in the young man's eyes at her bold answer and he threw back his head and laughed. "I am Tomlin," the knight

said, taking Janet's hands and spinning her round, "and today you shall stay here in the forest with me and we shall play."

All day long, Tomlin and Janet wandered through Carterhaugh Wood. They danced and sang and told each other stories. And by the evening, they were both deeply in love.

"I will not return to the castle without you," Janet vowed. "You must come with me and I will beg my father to let you stay."

"I cannot leave the wood," replied Tomlin sadly. "I was once human, but many years ago, when I was riding through the forest, the Fairy Queen caught me and enchanted me. Now I am an elf-knight, and I must ride by the side of the Fairy Queen to protect her for ever more. I only wish that I could be a man again, for then I would surely marry you."

"Is there no way to break the spell?" Janet sighed.

"There is," Tomlin said gently, "but you must be very brave."

"Tell me what I must do," Janet whispered.

"This very night is Halloween," Tomlin explained, "a night when fairies, goblins and witches ride abroad. You must go to Mile Cross and hide there until midnight, for then I will come riding by. First you will see a troop of riders on black horses. Then there will be a troop on brown horses. Next will come riders on horses as white as milk – and in the middle of them will ride the Fairy Queen herself. I will be among the elf-knights at her side, and I will wear only one glove so you can find me quickly among the throng. When you see me, you must run to my horse, seize its bridle and drag me down. You must then hold me fast, no matter what happens – for the fairy folk will cast all sorts of spells on me to try to keep me. If you have the strength and courage not to let go, the enchantment will at last be broken and I will be yours." Tomlin took Janet's hand. "Do you think you can do all this?" he asked quietly.

"Yes," breathed Janet. "Yes, I will."

Later that night, when everyone else was safely inside the castle with the doors and windows barred, Janet hid in the darkness on the moor at Mile Cross. Just before the stroke of midnight, she heard the thunder of hooves and out of the night appeared hundreds of black horses, bridles jangling and manes flying. On their backs were witches with bony fingers and sunken faces with dead, staring eyes.

Next, the brown horses galloped past, whinnying and snorting. The wrinkled goblins who rode them whipped them with willow switches and clutched the reins with wizened fingers.

Then the white horses came like glowing ghosts through the gloom, wild-eyed and foaming at the mouth, and at the centre of the riders Janet saw the beautiful Fairy Queen, sitting tall and fierce and proud. Quickly, Janet searched for a rider with only one glove. She plunged in among the pounding hooves, pulled down the enchanted elf-knight and held Tomlin to herself as tight as she could.

The Fairy Queen sent up an unearthly wail that tore through the darkness and all the hundreds of riders thundered around, shrieking and howling. Suddenly Janet felt Tomlin grow in her arms and she realised she was holding a huge, hairy bear. Still she held him fast, and he writhed into a hissing snake. Still she clutched him in her arms, and he bucked into an angry, snapping wolf. Still she held on tight, and he turned into a blazing branch that burnt into her flesh. Still Janet refused to let go, and in a flash of cold lightning she saw she was at last holding a naked, human man. As she wrapped Tomlin in her cloak, a haunting cry came from the Fairy Queen: "Tomlin, I would rather have changed your eyes to wood and your heart to stone than lost you!" Then suddenly the wild hunt was gone, disappeared into the night, and Janet and Tomlin were left alone on the dark, windy moor to make their way home to the castle together.

HOP-TOADS AND PEARLS

a retelling from the original tale by Charles Perrault

Go and fetch the water!" yelled the widow at her younger daughter. "You can finish that sweeping later! And hurry back with it. You've still got to light the fire and peel the potatoes for dinner."

The poor girl hurried to rest her broom in the corner and wipe her dusty hands on her tattered apron. She never grumbled about being treated like a slave because she was good and kind and couldn't think badly about anybody. But how she wished that her mother and her sister might help her out a little with all the housework now and again . . .

As the exhausted girl stumbled out to the well with the cumbersome bucket, the widow's elder daughter looked up from her comfy chair by the window and smirked. Fanchon was like her mother in every way: how she looked (very ugly), how she spoke (sharp and nasty) and how she acted (selfish and lazy). This was the reason why her mother adored her so: whenever she looked at Fanchon, she saw herself.

The widow's younger daughter reached the well and heaved up

a heavy, full bucket. Suddenly, she noticed that an old beggar-woman had joined her. The toothless crone wheezed, "My dear, I'm hoarse with thirst. Could you spare me a little drink?"

"Of course," the kind girl answered, and hurried to unhook the dripping bucket and help the beggar-woman to a ladleful.

Little did the younger daughter know that the hag who stood in front of her was actually a powerful fairy, who had disguised herself to put the girl to the test. The younger daughter kindly helped the beggar-woman to another ladleful of water and chatted politely to her for a while, before hauling the bucket back home.

How the girl's mother and her sister yelled and screamed and swore at her for taking so long at the well! "I do beg your pardon," the poor girl apologised. "I will be quicker next time." To everyone's surprise, a shining white pearl dropped from her lips with every word.

The stunned widow woman picked up a pearl from the floor, bit it hard between her teeth, and held it up to the light to examine it. "They're real!" she exclaimed, with a greedy twinkle in her eye. "What on earth happened at the well this evening? Tell me everything, or I'll lock you in the coal cellar all weekend."

The younger daughter was just as amazed as her mother and sister, and truthfully told them that she had done nothing but give a drink to a woman she'd met at the well. Pearls continued to drop from her lips as she spoke, and as fast as they fell, the widow scooped them up greedily into her pockets.

"Did you hear that, Fanchon?" she screeched delightedly. "Get yourself down to that well immediately!"

"Get lost!" the rude girl snorted. "I'm not fetching and carrying like a slave for anything!"

"I said GO!" the widow roared, cuffing the horrified Fanchon round the head. "Find that woman and give her a drink, whether she wants one or not! We're going to be rich, rich, rich! . . ."

Fanchon sulked and pouted, grumbled and cursed with every step that she lugged the splintery bucket – and it was only fear of her mother's temper that made her do it at all. She flung the bucket angrily into the well and moaned and groaned to herself with every wind as she pulled it back up. No sooner had she finished, than she noticed she had been joined by an elegant young woman dressed in fine robes. (It was the fairy again, but this time she had disguised herself as a princess.) "Good evening," the princess said politely, "would you be so good as to allow me a drink?"

"Oh, it's you, is it?" Fanchon sneered. "You're the reason why I've got splinters in my hands, splashes all over my dress, and my arms are killing me. You'd better make it worth my while and give me diamonds instead of pearls, that's all I can say." With that, Fanchon angrily flung the wooden ladle at the princess and dumped the bucket at her feet. "Go on then," she snapped.

No sooner had the princess taken one sip than Fanchon snatched the ladle back and humped the bucket back to the house. "There!" she yelled at her mother. "Happy now?" To everyone's horror, three great hop-toads leapt from her lips and sprang across the floor, croaking. Fanchon clapped her hands over her mouth in alarm.

"Whatever's happened?" cried the widow. "Where are the pearls?"

"I don't know!" wailed Fanchon, and three more hop-toads bounced, bulging-eyed, from her mouth. She began to scream and stamp her feet.

"This is all your fault, you ungrateful wretch!" the widow yelled at her younger daughter. She shoved the startled girl outside and slammed the door in her face. The poor younger daughter wandered off into the forest, sobbing . . .

The girl would almost certainly have got lost in the woods forever if the prince hadn't spotted her on his way back from a hunting trip. The prince was fascinated by the pearls that fell from her mouth, but he was even more charmed by the forgiving, kind way in which she spoke of her obviously horrible family. He took the lovely girl back to his palace at once, and after she had got to know and love him, he married her.

As for the nasty elder daughter, well, even her own mother tired of her moaning in the end. Besides, who wants to live with a house full of hop-toads? The widow threw the girl out, and they both lived the rest of their lives with only their miserable selves for company.

THE FIREBIRD

a Russian fairytale

Long ago in Russia, in the days when witches lurked in the forests and dragons flew over the plains and demons hid in the mountains, there lived a lord called Tsar Andronovich who owned a magnificent garden. At the centre of the garden lay a beautiful orchard, and in the middle of the orchard lay Tsar Andronovich's favourite tree – a tree which grew precious golden apples. Tsar Andronovich had given strict orders that no one was allowed to touch the golden apple tree except for himself. But one night, an amazing firebird with wings of flame and eyes of crystal came blazing into the orchard and stole some of the precious fruit.

"I must have this amazing firebird alive!" Tsar Andronovich marvelled. "This creature seems even more splendid than the golden apples she has been stealing!"

Half an hour later, the Tsar's three sons were galloping out of the gates in search of the firebird. The eldest and middle son, Dimitri and Vassili, thundered off together. They had teamed up to find the firebird and agreed to split their father's fortune between them. The youngest son, Ivan, was left to go off sadly on his own.

Ivan rode for three days and nights without any idea of where he was going and without seeing any sign of the firebird. His food and water began to run low and his horse was exhausted. Just as Ivan was thinking things couldn't get much worse, he heard a blood-curdling howl behind him and out of a dark forest ran a huge grey wolf. Ivan's horse shot away from under him, throwing him into the dirt. But it didn't escape very far. The grey wolf sprang onto it and gobbled it up.

"Eat me quickly and have done with it!" Ivan cried at the panting beast.

"I am not going to eat you," grinned the wolf. "I have to repay you for eating your very tasty horse! Now, I can't help noticing that you look worn out. Ride on me, the grey wolf. I will take you where you want to go."

Ivan was too tired and lonely to argue. He climbed onto the grey wolf's back and explained all about his quest to find the firebird. He had hardly finished speaking when the grey wolf leapt away like an arrow. It seemed like only a few seconds before they came to a halt before a stone wall.

"Ivan, climb over this wall and you will see the firebird in a golden cage," the wolf explained. "Take the firebird, but whatever you do, do not steal the golden cage."

Trembling, Ivan clambered over the wall and found himself in a courtyard below. Hanging from a tree in the middle was a golden cage with the firebird inside, just as the wolf had said. Ivan crept up to the leafy boughs, opened the jewelled door, and drew out the beautiful firebird. To his great surprise, she didn't flap or cry out or make any fuss at all. *Hmmm*, thought Ivan to himself. *I really need the cage as well, or else where am I going to keep the firebird?* He reached up into the leaves and unhooked the cage. At that very moment, ear-splitting alarm bells began to ring and guards rushed into the courtyard from all sides. They roughly dragged Ivan off to see their master, the Tsar Dolmat.

"You must pay dearly for trying to steal my precious firebird," boomed Tsar Dolmat, his face dark with anger. Then he rubbed his beard and thought for a second. "UNLESS," he added, "you go to the ends of the earth and bring me the horse with the golden mane. If you can do this, I will give you the firebird with pleasure."

Ivan crept back to the grey wolf hanging his head in shame. But his friend simply said, "Ride on me, the grey wolf, and I will take you where you want to go."

The grey wolf sprang away to the ends of the earth faster than the wind. It seemed like only a couple of minutes before they came to a stop outside some stables.

"Ivan, go into these stables and take the horse with the golden mane," the wolf told him. "But whatever you do, do not steal its golden bridle."

Cautiously, Ivan edged into the stables, crept up to the horse with the golden mane, and began to lead it out of its stall. *Hmmm,* thought Ivan, as he looked at its golden bridle hanging on the wall. *I really need the bridle as well, or else how am I going to ride the horse?* The moment he lifted down the bridle a clanging peal of bells broke the silence. Soldiers dashed into the stable and hauled Ivan away to see their master, the Tsar Afron.

"You must pay dearly for trying to steal my wonderful horse with the golden mane," raged Tsar Afron, shaking with fury. "UNLESS," he added, "you go to the other side of the world and bring me Tasha the Beautiful to be my bride. If you can do this, I will gladly give you the horse with the golden mane."

Ivan could hardly bring himself to tell the grey wolf that he had disobeyed him a second time. But when the wolf saw Ivan returning empty-handed he simply said, "Ride on me, the grey wolf, and I will take you where you want to go."

Ivan jumped onto the grey wolf and he sped away to the other side of the world as quick as lightning. It seemed like only an hour or so before they drew up outside a glorious palace.

"Ivan, this time I am going to be the one who goes inside and you are going to be the one who waits," said the wolf and he sprang over the palace wall with one mighty bound. Ivan hardly had time to draw breath before the wolf came springing over again – this time with Tasha the Beautiful tossed onto his back. Ivan leapt onto the wolf's back and they were off through the air like a shooting star.

By the time the three
arrived back at Tsar
Afron's home, the grey
wolf was highly surprised
to find Ivan weeping bitterly.

"Why are you crying?"
the grey wolf asked. "If we
give Tasha the Beautiful to Tsar
Afron, you will get the horse with the
golden mane. If we give the horse with the
golden mane to Tsar Dolmat, you will get the firebird. If we give the
firebird to Tsar Andronovich, your father, you will get all the wealth
he possesses."

"But I have fallen in love with Tasha," Ivan protested, "and she
has fallen in love with me!"

The grey wolf looked at Tasha the Beautiful and she nodded
sadly, biting her lip.

"Oh very well," sighed the grey wolf. "I will turn myself into
the form of Tasha the Beautiful. You can present me to Tsar Afron in
her place and he will give you the horse with the golden mane. When
you are safely two mountains away, think of me, the grey wolf, and I
will be back at your side."

And so it all happened. Tsar Afron was tricked and soon Ivan
was once again mounted on the grey wolf while his sweetheart Tasha
the Beautiful rode prettily on the horse with the golden mane.

As they drew near the villa of Tsar Dolmat, Ivan sighed a deep
sigh. "Oh grey wolf," he began, "I would so like to keep this horse
with a golden mane. Would you turn into the form of the horse, as
you disguised yourself as Tasha before? Then I could take you to Tsar

Dolmat and win the firebird. When I am safely two forests away, I will think of you and you will return back to my side."

The grey wolf looked at Ivan and bowed slightly. "For you, I will do this," said the wolf gruffly. And so it all came to pass. Tsar Dolmat was tricked, and Ivan was once again mounted on the grey wolf while his sweetheart Tasha the Beautiful rode prettily on the horse with the golden mane and carried the firebird.

By and by, the companions came to the very spot where the grey wolf had set upon Ivan's horse and eaten it. Then it was the grey wolf's turn to sigh a deep sigh. "Well, Ivan, here I took a horse from you and here I now return you with another horse – and a beautiful bride and a firebird, too! You no longer need me and I must go!" And the wolf loped off into the woods and was gone.

Ivan and Tasha went on their way in sadness, weeping for their lost friend. When they were very nearly back home at Tsar Andronovich's house, they stopped to rest and sank into an exhausted sleep. Even the firebird was so soundly asleep that she didn't notice two figures come creeping out of the shadows. It was Dimitri and Vassily, who had returned from their travels empty handed and were enraged to find their little brother not only with the firebird but also with Tasha the Beautiful! In their bitterness, the brothers drew their swords and stabbed Ivan where he lay dreaming. Then they swept up Tasha the Beautiful and the firebird and were off to their father's mansion, to pretend that the treasures were theirs. "Breathe a word of this and we'll kill you," they hissed into Tasha's ear, and Tasha shook with sorrow and fear . . .

Ivan's body lay lifeless and cold as snow started to cover him like a thick blanket. A few bold birds and woodland creatures began to creep closer to find out what type of thing would lie so silent and still in the freezing weather – and among them came a grey wolf with yellow eyes and drooling jaws. He stalked right up to Ivan's body and sniffed all round. Then he sat in the snow, threw his head back and howled a spine-chilling howl. Slowly and gently the wolf began to lick the wound in Ivan's chest. And suddenly, Ivan sat up and began to shiver. "What am I doing asleep in this snowstorm?" he asked the grey wolf.

"Ride on me, the grey wolf," came the gruff voice, "and I will take you where you want to go."

"Home," whispered Ivan into his friend's ear, "I want to go home." And no sooner had he finished saying the words than they were there.

Of course, when Tsar Andronovich learnt the truth, he threw the wicked Dimitri and Vassily in a dungeon, where they belonged. Ivan and Tasha the Beautiful were married – Ivan rode his faithful grey wolf to the wedding ceremony and Tasha arrived on the horse with the golden mane. As for Tsar Andronovich, well he got his precious firebird after all – and he loved her so much he even let her eat the golden apples from his favourite tree whenever she wanted.

THE RED SHOES

retold from the original tale by Hans Christian Andersen

There was once a woman who was so poor that she couldn't afford to buy her daughter, Karen, any shoes. The woman often wept to see Karen's feet all rough and blistered. She would have been overjoyed to know that the shoemaker's wife felt so sorry for Karen that she was making her a pair of red shoes from some of her husband's left-over leather. But the woman never found out. She died the very day that the red shoes were finished and Karen wore them for the first time as she walked behind her mother's coffin on the way to church.

The shoemaker's wife couldn't sew very well and the shoes had turned out to be rather clumsy and misshapen. But Karen thought that her soft, red shoes were the most wonderful things in all the world. However, the old lady who kindly took Karen in said, "You can't possibly go walking around in those odd things. Whatever will people think?" She threw the red shoes onto the fire and bought Karen a pair of sensible, sturdy black ones.

It was the sensible, sturdy black shoes that Karen was wearing when the old lady took her to the palace to see the parade for the little princess's birthday. The king and queen stood with the little princess on the balcony, waving and smiling. But Karen didn't look at the gracious expressions on their faces, or their fine rich robes. Karen couldn't take her eyes off the red shoes on the little princess's feet. They were magnificent – made out of satin instead of leather, so they actually shone like rubies. *Those really are the most wonderful things in all the world*, thought Karen.

From that moment, whenever Karen buckled on her sensible, black shoes, she thought of the little princess's beautiful red ones. Whenever Karen took off her sensible black shoes, she thought of the princess's beautiful red ones. And she longed for those beautiful red shoes with all her heart.

One day, the old lady who looked after Karen looked at her sensible,black shoes and tutted, "My, my! Those are looking rather old and shabby – and they're too small for you now. We can't have you going along to church in those tomorrow." The old lady handed her a purse full of money. "Buy yourself some new ones," she smiled.

Karen walked all the way to the shoe shop with a thumping heart. First, she tried on some sensible, sturdy black shoes – but there were none to fit her. Then she tried on some smart, lace-up brown shoes – but they still either slopped up and down or cramped her toes. Then Karen peered up at a high shelf and saw a red pair exactly like the ones the little princess had worn. They fitted her perfectly. Karen held her breath as she handed over her money and stepped out of the shop. Her feet gleamed and twinkled in the sunlight. She could hardly believe it. Her dream had come true.

Karen knew full well that the old lady wouldn't approve at all of her choice. But luckily for her, the old lady's eyesight wasn't what it was, and the colour of Karen's new shoes was just a dark blur. Karen kept quiet, saying nothing of the truth.

Next day, Karen's heart nearly burst with excitement as she slipped on her red shoes. She tripped gaily all the way to church, and even though it was a beautiful day and there were many finely dressed people about, she had eyes for no one and nothing except the red shoes. She twisted and turned as she walked, so her toes and heels shone in turn. She hoped that everyone would see them.

Even when Karen was sitting in her church pew, she couldn't take her eyes off her red shoes. Even when the priest was praying, she couldn't

take her eyes off her red shoes. Even when the organist began to strike up a joyful hymn of praise, she couldn't take her eyes off the red shoes. The statues of the angels and saints seemed to frown down sternly upon her, but Karen didn't notice. She still couldn't take her eyes off the red shoes.

As the choir started to sing out and their voices filled the air, Karen felt a strange sensation in her feet. Her toes began to twitch inside the red satin. Her heels began to quiver to and fro. Suddenly, Karen's feet began to dance. Right there and then in church, Karen's red shoes forced her to stand up and leap and turn and skip. With the eyes of the whole congregation staring at her, Karen's red shoes danced her down the aisle and out into the sunlight. "Help me!" she cried, but no one knew what to do. The red shoes danced Karen all around the graveyard and out of the church gate. Then they danced her round and round the churchyard wall and off down the street . . .

By day and by night, the enchanted red shoes carried Karen along, twinkling wickedly. They danced her in and out of houses and up and down stairs. They danced her right through the city gates across the fields and into the dark forest. They danced her out of the trees and through meadows, until Karen had quite forgotten how long she had been dancing . . . and still they made Karen dance. "Forgive me!" the sobbing girl cried out. "Forgive me for thinking of these foolish pretty things above everything else!" At last, the red shoes were still. Utterly exhausted, Karen collapsed into a heap and closed her eyes. And when her soul reached heaven, she never had to dance or think about red shoes ever again.

THE MAGIC TINDERBOX

retold from the original tale by Hans Christian Andersen

A soldier came marching down the road – left, right! left, right! left, right!

"Good morning, sir," croaked an ugly witch sitting at the roadside. "If you do as I say, I will make you very rich. You see that huge tree there –" the witch pointed over to an old oak – "it is quite hollow." You must climb to the top, wriggle through a hole and then lower yourself down the inside of the trunk all the way to the bottom. You will see three doors. Open the first one and you will find yourself inside a room where a frightening dog sits on a box full of money. Spread my blue-and-white checked apron on the floor, put the dog onto it, and he won't bother you at all. Then you can open the box and take out as much money as you can carry. In this first room, the money will be copper. If you'd rather have silver, you must face the even scarier dog in the second room. If you'd prefer gold, you must go into the third room – but there the dog is yet more terrifying."

"What do you want for yourself?" the soldier grinned.

"I don't want a single coin of the money," the witch cackled. "Just bring me a rusty old tinderbox that my granny forgot last time she was in there."

"Very well," agreed the soldier, and the witch gave him her apron. Then the soldier shimmied up the outside of the old oak tree, wriggled through the hole, and lowered himself down . . . down . . . down the inside. He found himself in a long corridor lit by one hundred burning lanterns, and sure enough, there were three doors in front of him. The soldier bravely put his hand on the first doorknob and turned it.

"Great Scott!" he cried, springing back in alarm. There in the middle of the room was a dog with eyes the size of teacups. The soldier tore his eyes away from its staring gaze, lay the witch's apron on the floor and lifted the dog on to it. Then he unlocked the box the dog had been sitting on. Amazing! It was filled to the brim with shining copper coins. The soldier gleefully grabbed huge handfuls and stuffed them into his knapsack, his pockets and even his boots.

The second dog couldn't possibly have eyes bigger than that first one, the soldier thought to himself. Boldly, he walked to the second doorknob and turned it . . .

"Good lord!" he yelled. There in the middle of the room was a dog with eyes the size of mill-wheels. Round and round and round they churned – it made you dizzy just to look at them. Once again, the soldier forced himself to look away. He laid the witch's apron down, heaved the dog onto it, and unlocked the box on which it had been sitting. Fantastic! There before him was a treasure trove of silver! The soldier got rid of all the copper coins quick as quick and filled his knapsack, pockets and boots.

"Surely the third dog's eyes can't be any bigger than that!" the soldier said to himself, laughing at his good luck. He went to the third doorknob and turned it . . .

"Heavens above!" he cried. The third dog had eyes the size of the Round Tower of the city of Copenhagen. Not only that, but they whizzed round and round in his head like Catherine Wheels. It was several minutes before the soldier found he could look at something other than the dog's enormous spinning eyeballs. Then he laid down the witch's apron, hauled the dog onto it, and unlocked the box it had been sitting on. Unbelievable! There was enough gold to buy the palace of the King of Denmark himself! Chortling with joy, the soldier emptied his knapsack, pockets and boots of every last silver coin and crammed them with gold instead. He hurried off down the corridor, found the tinderbox, and then climbed up . . . up . . . up and out of the tree.

"Where's my tinderbox then?" the witch cackled.

"Tell me why you want it so badly and I'll give it to you," replied the soldier, firmly.

"Where IS IT?" the witch shrieked in annoyance.

"If you don't tell me why you want it, I'll cut off your head," insisted the soldier.

"GIVE ME MY TINDERBOX!" the witch howled in frustration.

"Very well," said the soldier, and he drew his sword and cut off the witch's head. Then he went on his merry way down the road, with his knapsack, pockets and boots weighed down with gold, and the witch's tinderbox tucked safely inside his jacket.

At the very next
town, the soldier
booked into the best hotel, ate in
the most expensive restaurant, and went to the
most exclusive shop to buy himself new clothes. At once the soldier
found he had a lot of new friends and they told him of all the
wonders to be seen in the town – particularly the beautiful princess,
who lived in the castle on top of the hill.

"How can I get to see this princess?" the soldier asked.

"You can't," his new friends explained, "no one can. For it has
been prophesied that she will one day marry a common soldier, and
the king and queen keep the princess locked up so this can never
happen."

Day after day, the soldier spent his gold on the finest things
money could buy for himself and his friends. It was a horrible shock
when he went one morning to fill his pockets and found that all the
gold was gone. Suddenly, the soldier's friends disappeared. The
soldier had to move out of the grand hotel and into a dingy attic at
the top of fourteen flights of stairs. He didn't even have enough
money for a candle to cheer things up with a bit of light. Then the

soldier remembered the witch's tinderbox. Surely he could use that to give him a few sparks to start a warming fire? No sooner had the soldier struck the tinderbox once with the flint than there was a flash of lightning and the dog with eyes the size of teacups appeared.

"What is your command, sir?" the dog growled, bowing its head respectfully.

Once the soldier had got over the shock, he stammered, "Well, I suppose I'd really like you to get me some money."

The dog immediately vanished – but reappeared an instant later with a purse of money clamped between its jaws.

The soldier whooped and danced about with delight. Suddenly he understood the secret of the tinderbox. Strike it once, twice or three times, and the dog from the first, second or third room appeared to grant his wishes!

Soon the soldier was richer than ever. He moved back into the grand hotel, ate at the expensive restaurant once again, bought himself new suits of fine clothes, and found himself surrounded by friends once more. He had everything he could wish for – except for a wife to share it all with. *That princess must be very bored locked up there in the castle,* the soldier thought to himself.

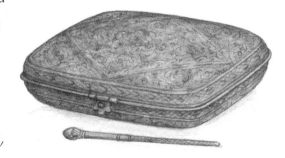

The soldier waited till it was dark, then struck the tinderbox once. In a flash, the dog with the eyes like teacups appeared. "I would like to see the beautiful princess," the soldier said. Before he could blink, the dog ran off and then reappeared with the princess lying on its broad back, fast asleep. She was indeed very beautiful and the soldier couldn't resist bending over to give her a kiss. The dog then disappeared and the princess was gone.

Next morning, up in the castle on the hill, the princess remembered what had happened as if it had been a strange dream, and she told her mother and father all about it. The king and queen were deeply worried. The clever queen sewed a pretty silk bag, filled it with flour and tied it around her daughter's neck when she went to bed. Then the queen pierced a tiny hole in the bag, tucked the princess in and kissed her goodnight.

Of course, the soldier had fallen deeply in love with the princess and that night he sent the dog to fetch her again. Neither the dog nor the soldier noticed the thin line of flour that ran down from the silk bag and left a tell-tale trail all the way from the castle to his door. And in the morning, when the princess was safely back in her bed, the soldier was woken by royal officers breaking down his door. They grabbed him and dragged him away to be hanged.

A huge crowd of townspeople had gathered to watch the soldier die, and opposite the gallows sat the smug king and queen and all the members of the town council. Just as the hangman put the noose around the soldier's neck, the desperate man had an idea. "Will you grant me one last wish?" he yelled out to the king. "I would like to smoke a pipe of tobacco before I die."

The king thought for a moment. He didn't want to seem merciless in front of all the people, so, "Very well," he said. To the soldier's great delight, the hangman untied his hands and offered him a pipe and some matches.

"Don't worry," the soldier grinned, "I have my own light," and he pulled out his tinderbox and struck it three times.

At once, the dog with the eyes as big as teacups, the dog with the eyes as big as mill-wheels, and the dog with the eyes as big as the

Round Tower of the city of Copenhagen stood before him. "Save me," the soldier cried, "or I will surely die!" The dogs growled like rumbling thunder and sprang among the crowd, scattering them everywhere in terror. They made straight for the king and queen and the table of town councillors. One by one, the dogs picked them up in their jaws and hurled them far, far away over the most distant hills. "Hooray!" the townspeople cried. "We never liked them anyway. We'd much prefer the brave soldier to be our king and the beautiful princess to be our queen!" And that's exactly what happened. They were married straight away – and the three dogs were guests of honour at the wedding feast.

THE CLOTH OF DREAMS

by Jenny Koralek

There was once a boy who was getting ready to visit his grandmother, when he tripped on his cloth of dreams and tore it. His grandmother had made the cloth of dreams and spread it over his cradle when he was born.

"It will keep the dark night things away," she said to his mother, "but only, of course, until he is big enough to forge his own courage."

Thanks to the cloth of dreams the boy had never yet known a bad night, but there it now lay with two large holes in it.

"Never mind," said his mother. "Give it to your grandmother and she will most surely mend it."

But when the boy got to his grandmother's house he forgot all about the torn cloth of dreams.

In the garden the swing was waiting for him under the apple tree, the doves were calling to be fed, the goldfish were blowing bubbles in the lilypond and the sundial was telling him it was supper time.

In the kitchen the table creaked with all his favourite food, salty and spicy, sugary and sweet, hot and cold and fizzy. In the bedroom the pillows were punchy, the mattress was bouncy and when he drew the cloth of dreams up to his chin, his grandmother lit a candle and told him the kind of stories he liked best, stories with rhyme and without reason.

So of course the boy forgot all about the torn cloth of dreams. But his grandmother had seen the holes and, as she made her way to her room, smiled sadly to herself.

When the boy fell asleep with moonlight on his face, a chain of nightmares came out through the holes in the cloth of dreams and, as they were new to him, he was quite helpless in front of them.

A frightful hag chased him through a wood full of leafless trees with branches like claws and caught him and tickled him with long, stabbing, bony fingers. He pulled himself away, but no sooner was he free than he fell into the jaws of a huge fish. Down he fell into its hot, steamy belly, which was so big the boy could stand up in it. He shouted and shouted for his grandmother but no sounds came out of his mouth. When at last the fish opened its toothy jaws the boy fell out with a crash and landed on a frozen puddle.

Suddenly he woke up and found he was lying on the floor shivering with the torn cloth of dreams beside him. Then he remembered the holes and what his mother had said to him: "Give it to your grandmother and she will most surely mend it."

So the boy picked up the cloth of dreams and opened the door of his bedroom. But oh! How dark the landing was, how big and dark. The moon had disappeared behind a huge cloud, his grandmother had taken the candle with her and if there were other lights the boy did not know how to find them. He could see the light glowing beneath his grandmother's door, but that only made things worse because he could make out shapes all round him, uncertain shapes which might be the things that were there in the day but might be things which came in the night.

The boy was afraid to turn back and afraid to go on. His body trembled and his teeth chattered but he fixed his eyes on the glow from his grandmother's room and set forth with his fears across the dark, shape-filled landing. He stubbed his toes on one strange thing and hit his elbow on another. Each step he took made a fearful creak, something sighed in the curtains and for a moment he lost sight of the light.

But suddenly he was there in the doorway of his grandmother's glowing room, holding out the torn cloth of dreams.

"Horrible things came through these holes," he said, "and I made a dark crossing to come to you. Please will you mend it?"

"With your help," said his grandmother, "I most surely will."

And she picked up an empty basket and led him to a little door that he had not seen before and set him on a steep stairway.

"You must fetch me threads from the sun and threads from the moon," said grandmother.

"B-but," stammered the boy.

"No buts," said grandmother. "I am too old to climb the stairs."

Gripped with fear the boy climbed the stairs one by one and came out onto a flat place on the roof which seemed to be touching the sky. The silver moon was fading into a green sky and the golden sun was rising into a rosy sky and the boy had never before seen anything so beautiful and powerful, so quiet and so certain. All the same he was terrified. Surely the sun would burn him. Surely the moon would freeze him. But surely his grandmother would not let harm come to him. After all, it was she who had made the cloth of dreams to protect him.

So the boy put out a brave hand and pulled at the sun's first rays, which he found were as warm as his grandmother's smile. Then he pulled at the moon's last rays, which he found to be as cold and as sharp as his fears in the dark, but he went on standing there firmly in his bare feet, pulling at the rays until the basket was full. Then he bounded down the stairs and gave it to his grandmother.

In the twinkling of an eye she threaded the gold and threaded the silver and flashed her needle through the cloth of dreams and suddenly the gaping holes disappeared.

"There you are," said his grandmother, holding out the cloth of dreams. "Not that you need it now. Tonight you have forged your own courage. Now you are your own true sword and will know how to do battle with night and day and light and dark and smiles and frowns and fears and joys."

"Will I?" asked the boy in a whisper.

"You will," said the grandmother.

And they smiled at one another.

Then, as the world was stepping out of night into a new day, the boy ran downstairs two at a time, out to the garden and across the dewy grass. Onto the swing he jumped and swung it high, higher than he had ever before.

Favourites

SEVEN AT ONE BLOW
a traditional folk tale

There was once a little tailor who was a very cheeky chap. Maybe he was a cheeky chap *because* he was little, I don't know. In any case, he was little and he was cheeky and he was a tailor – and that's the truth of it.

The little cheeky tailor was sewing one day and nibbling on a thick slice of bread and jam (it was strawberry – his favourite) when several big fat flies started buzzing round the jam pot. "Get lost!" he spluttered through a mouthful of crumbs. "Buzz off!" He flicked at the flies with his sewing, but the stubborn insects just buzzed round the jam pot more determinedly than ever. "I'll show you!" the little cheeky tailor murmured, and he jumped down from his sewing stool and fetched his broom from the corner. Very slowly (so as not to arouse the flies' suspicion), he lifted his broom high above his head and – THWACK! – brought it down swift and hard right on top of the jam pot. When the little cheeky tailor looked underneath, his chest puffed up with pride. "Well, look at that!" he crowed. "I've killed seven at one blow! What a hero I am!"

The little cheeky tailor put aside his work, found some silver material, and quickly ran himself up a wide belt. He decorated it with sparkly glass beads and embroidered it in gold thread with the words: SEVEN AT ONE BLOW. Then the little cheeky tailor buckled it around his waist and stood in front of the mirror. *"My, my!"* he breathed. "What's a splendid champion like me doing in a dingy little workroom like this? I should be out and about in public, so everyone can admire me!" With that, the little cheeky tailor left his sewing shop for the last time and set off down the road, humming merrily to himself and tipping his hat politely to all he met.

It wasn't long before everyone was gossiping about the hero who had killed seven at one blow. "Just imagine slaying seven men at one blow!" the people exclaimed.

"No, it wasn't seven men," others insisted, "it was seven trolls!" "You are wrong," yet more protested. "It wasn't seven trolls, it was seven dragons!"

Eventually, even the king got to hear of the very small, but very brave, champion and he ordered him to the palace at once.

"You see, my problem is this," the king explained, bending low so that he could see eye to eye with the little cheeky tailor. "There are two giants who keep robbing my villages and killing my subjects. If you get rid of them, I'll give you half of my kingdom."

"And . . ." said the little cheeky tailor (because he was very cheeky like that).

"And what?" said the king, very puzzled.

"And your daughter's hand in marriage," chuckled the little cheeky tailor. "It's only usual in cases like this."

"Oh very well," grumbled the king, "I'll throw in my daughter's hand in marriage, too."

"Very well," chirped the little cheeky tailor. "Two giants mean nothing to me. Don't forget that I have killed seven at one blow." And with a wink he strode off, his belt sparkling in the sunlight.

When the little cheeky tailor found the giants, they were both asleep under a huge, shady oak tree. The little cheeky tailor patted his belt comfortingly, picked up two large, round pebbles, and tucked them into his shirt. Then he tried to creep up to the tree. He had problems getting close, because each time he walked forward, the giants' enormous snores blew him back. Finally, he made a mad run for it and – looking a little windswept – reached the trunk. He climbed nimbly into the branches and chuckled to himself. Then – PLOP! – he threw one of the stones down at the first sleeping giant and hit him smack on the nose.

"OY!" roared the giant, waking up at once and turning on his brother. "What did you do that for, dungbreath?"

"Do what?" mumbled the second dozing giant.

"You know!" bellowed the first giant. "Just don't do it again!" And he settled back to sleep.

High up in the tree, the little cheeky tailor giggled and dropped his other stone. PLOP! Again, it hit the first giant's conk.

"OY!" he boomed, sitting bolt upright and glaring at his brother. "I told you not to do that, thunderpants!" And he socked the second giant right in the mush.

"What on earth did you do that for, mouldybeard?" the wounded giant roared, and he punched his brother in the mouth.

That was the start of a giant fight that raged so hard and long the people in the nearby village thought there was an earthquake. The little cheeky tailor was very nearly shaken out of the oak tree, but at the end of it, the giants both lay dead beneath him and he had nothing worse than a bruised bottom.

And that is how a little tailor came to win half a kingdom and marry a princess all through being a very cheeky chap. Maybe he was a cheeky chap *because* he was little, I don't know. In any case, he was little and he was cheeky and he was a tailor – and that's the truth.

ALI BABA AND THE FORTY THIEVES
a tale from The Arabian Nights

Listen, O my beloved, and I will tell you the tale of a man called Ali Baba. Ali Baba worked as a woodcutter and was as poor and generous as his merchant brother, Kasim, was rich and mean. But the time came when Allah (may His name be praised forever!) smiled on Ali Baba and changed his fortunes forever.

Late one afternoon, the woodcutter was leading his pack mules down a rocky valley when he saw a cloud of dust in the distance, approaching fast. Ali Baba hurried to hide himself and his mules among the cliffs, where he could peep out unseen from behind a boulder. It wasn't long before forty horses carrying forty bandits came thundering into the valley, led by an ugly robber chief on a jet-black stallion. Ali Baba's legs turned to jelly as the vicious-looking thugs slid off their wild-eyed horses and walked straight towards the rock face. The robber chief suddenly cried, "Open sesame!" and to the woodcutter's utter amazement, the rock split in two with a groan, leaving an opening in the cliff. The robber chief and his men strode straight inside and the rocks clashed together behind them. Ali Baba was left in the silence of the valley, listening to the whinnying of the

horses and the pounding of his own
heart. ·

After what seemed like ages
(although Ali Baba knew it must
only be a few minutes), the men
reappeared, each carrying a heavy
saddlebag. "Yalla!" cried the
robber chief, and he and his
bandits jumped onto their
stamping steeds and raced away,
leaving a whirlwind of dust behind
them.

"May Allah be merciful!"
gasped Ali Baba, and he scrambled
down the cliff face as fast as his short
legs would carry him. "Open sesame!" he cried, as
loud as he could manage. The cliff face split asunder and revealed the
entrance to a huge cavern filled with treasure from years of bandit
raiding. Jewelled swords and golden plates and silver lanterns hung
from the walls. Earrings and necklaces and bracelets spilled out from
huge chests. Rolls of expensive silks were stacked up next to jars
containing precious spices. And gold coins spilled onto the cavern
floor from thousands of overflowing sacks.

Ali Baba stood open-mouthed for just a few seconds. Then he
sprang into the cave and the rocks smashed shut behind him.
Working quickly, Ali Baba filled his pockets and some empty sacks
with coins and other treasures. "Open sesame!" he cried again, and to
his great relief the entrance reappeared. He hauled his booty outside
and loaded up his mules while the rocks slid seamlessly together. Ali

Baba hurried home under cover of darkness, murmuring prayers of gratitude all the way.

Being a good, generous man, the first thing Ali Baba did after telling his wife about his good fortune was to tell his brother and offer to share half of his treasure with him. But being a jealous, greedy man, this wasn't enough for Kasim. He insisted that Ali Baba describe to him exactly where to find the magical cliff and exactly how to open the entrance.

At first light the very next day, Kasim rode out to find the bandits' cavern for himself. He arrived at the rock face, cried "Open sesame!" and ran delightedly into the treasure cave. But when he had filled all his bags to bursting and it was time to go, Kasim began to panic. "Open barley!" he cried – nothing happened. "Open wheat!" – again, nothing. Kasim knew that the magic word was some type of cereal, but he couldn't for the life of him remember which. "Open oats!" he tried, and "Open maize!" –

but not even as much as a fine crack appeared in the rock. As Kasim sat dejectedly on the cavern floor he felt the ground underneath him tremble. A few seconds later, the cliff in front of him opened with a crack of thunder. The robber chief and his bandits had returned . . .

As you can imagine, O my beloved, Kasim did not return home that night . . . nor the next . . . nor the next. And when Ali Baba went searching in the valley for his brother, he found Kasim's body displayed inside the robbers' cave in four bits. Now, as everyone knows, all good people like to be buried in one piece. So the grieving Ali Baba took home Kasim's remains and paid a tailor to come blindfolded to his house and sew the pieces of his brother back together without asking any awkward questions.

Of course, as soon as the bandits returned to their treasure cave and found the pieces of their victim missing, they realised that someone else knew the whereabouts of their lair and the all-important magic password. "We will search every street in Arabia until we find this intruding dog!" the robber chief roared, and the bandits galloped off at once.

It was the robber chief himself who made the all-important discovery. Lurking in the marketplace just before dawn, he stopped and admired the nimble work of a tailor who was already at his stall and sewing in the half-light.

"This is nothing!" laughed the tailor. "Last week I had to sew a man's dead body together with my eyes covered!"

At that, the robber chief grabbed the tailor by the scruff of the neck and lifted him into the air with one hand. "Show me where you did this, or I'll personally turn you into a human pin-cushion," the robber chief growled.

"Whatever you say," gasped the tailor, "but I was blindfolded, so I'll have to try to remember the way with my eyes shut."

The tailor screwed his eyes up tight and groped his way through the streets all the way to Ali Baba's front door.

"Are you sure this is the one?" spat the robber chief.

"May the fleas of a thousand camels infest my armpits if I am wrong," gulped the tailor.

So the robber chief marked Ali Baba's door with a tiny red cross and disappeared into the morning hustle and bustle.

That night, a merchant with a train of mules carrying forty huge jars of oil came knocking at Ali Baba's door, asking for shelter for the night. Little did Ali Baba know that the merchant was really the robber chief in disguise. And never could he have guessed that only one of the jars actually contained oil. Hidden inside the other thirty-nine jars were the remaining thirty-nine bandits, waiting to jump out whenever the robber chief gave the word and slay everyone in Ali Baba's household!

Ever-generous, Ali Baba welcomed the merchant into his house and told his servants to set the oil jars down in his courtyard. Soon the robber chief found himself sitting at his sworn-enemy's table, being served a delicious feast.

While Ali Baba entertained his guest, his slave girl, Maryam, ran back and forth in the kitchen preparing dish after dish of tasty food. Half-way through the cooking she realised with a shock that she had run out of oil – then heaved a sigh of relief as she remembered all the jars of oil out in the yard. *Surely my master's guest won't mind if I take a little of his oil in return for our hospitality,* Maryam thought to herself.

As soon as Maryam's footsteps padded close to the first jar, she was shocked to hear a voice hissing at her from within: "Is it time yet?" Now Maryam was a clever girl, and she realised at once that the merchant and his oil jars could not possibly be what they seemed. "No, not yet," Maryam replied into the air hole in the lid, in as deep a voice as she could manage, and she passed onto the next jar. Again the same thing happened . . . and again as she approached the third jar – and every time until she reached the fortieth jar. Then she realised who the oil merchant really was and what exactly was inside his thirty-nine jars of oil!

Quickly and quietly, the brave girl dragged the fortieth jar into the kitchen and poured the oil into a huge kettle that hung over the fire. As soon as the oil was smoking and boiling away, Maryam filled a large pitcher and poured the burning liquid into the air holes of all thirty-nine jars. "Ha!" she said, as the last of the boiling oil trickled away. "That's the end of you lot!"

Next Maryam hurried to her chamber and dressed in her dancing costume. How beautiful she looked, wrapped in her coloured scarves and tinkling with golden chains and sequins! And how she delighted Ali Baba and his guest when she made her entrance, elegantly twirling to the music. The so-called oil merchant grinned a toothy smile and beckoned for Maryam to come closer . . . and closer . . . He was still smiling when Maryam floated right up beside him, swiftly pulled a silver dagger out from under her costume and stabbed it down hard through his heart.

Ali Baba jumped to his feet and tore at his hair in shock. "Look what you've done!" he howled. "You've killed our guest! Surely you will bring down the wrath of Allah upon us!" But Maryam whipped off the oil merchant's false beard and eyebrows, and stripped him of his turban and his robes – and there lay the robber chief, cold and still.

"But – how –" spluttered Ali Baba, and Maryam grabbed him by the hand, led him out into the courtyard and uncovered the dead thirty-nine robbers in the oil jars.

Ali Baba was so grateful that he gave Maryam her freedom at once. She married his son and became a proper member of the family. With the forty thieves out of the way, Ali Baba was the only person in the whole world who knew the whereabouts of the bandits' treasure cave and the magic words, "Open sesame". He and his family shared a lot of their riches among the poor, as Allah in heaven wants us all to do. But there was more than enough left over for Ali Baba and his family to live in happiness and wealth for the rest of their lives.

THE LITTLE MATCHGIRL

retold from the original tale by Hans Christian Andersen

It was New Year's Eve and bitterly cold. Snow and ice lined the streets like an untrodden white carpet, for all the people were indoors, happily preparing to bring in the New Year. All alone in the windy square by the fountain, the poor girl who sold matches shivered. She pulled her ragged shawl a little closer around her thin cotton dress. She rubbed her hands together and blew on her fingers and stamped her feet, but freezing wet snow came swamping through the holes in her boots.

The little matchgirl hadn't sold one box of matches all day and she was too frightened to go home, for her father would be extremely angry. "Someone will surely pass this way and buy in a minute," she told herself. But how cold she was, how cold! "If only I could light one of my matches," she murmured, "that would warm me a little." With fingers stiff with cold, the little matchgirl falteringly took out one of her matches and struck it.

The tiny wooden splinter blazed into a bright little flame and the little matchgirl cupped her hands over it, craving its spark of warmth and light. As she stared into the orange centre of the flame, she saw herself standing in front of a roaring stove, giving out heat that warmed her from the tips of her toes to the top of her head. Suddenly, the match's flame went out and the vision died with it. The little matchgirl somehow felt even colder than before.

The little matchgirl didn't dare light another match for a long time. Then "Just one more," she whispered, through her chattering teeth. Shaking, the little matchgirl drew out another of her precious wares and struck it on the wall. The glimmer from the little matchstick seemed to light up the stone until it was clear and glassy, like a crystal window. Through the window, the little matchgirl could see a room with a welcoming fire and bright candles and a table laden with delicious things to eat, and she held out her hands towards it. It seemed as if she was going to be able to reach right through the glass and into the wonderful room – then the match died out. The magical room vanished, and huge tears filled the little matchgirl's eyes.

Her poor numb hands fumbled to light another, and her pale face lit up with wonder in the glow of the third flame. Suddenly a

magnificent Christmas tree sparkled before the little matchgirl in the light. It shimmered with glassy balls of many colours and glittered with tinsel, and tiny dots of candlelight danced all over its thick green needles. "How beautiful!" breathed the little matchgirl, her eyes big and round. Then the match scorched her fingers and she dropped it, black and twisted, into the snow. The Christmas tree was gone, but the glimmering lights from its candles were still there, rising up and up into the night sky until they mingled with the twinkling stars. Suddenly, one of the lights fell through the darkness, leaving a blazing trail of silver behind it. "That means someone is dying," the little matchgirl murmured, remembering what her Granny used to say whenever they saw shooting stars.

As the little matchgirl stood dreaming of her beloved, dead grandmother, she unthinkingly lit up another match – and there was her granny before her in the light of the flame. "Granny, don't go!" sobbed the little matchgirl, as she lit one match after another, so the vision wouldn't fade like all the others. "Let me stay with you!" she begged, and the old lady smiled and held out her arms for the little matchgirl to run into, just as she always had done.

It was midnight, and all over the city the church bells pealed out to welcome in the New Year. Revellers poured out of the inns and houses to dance and sing and shake hands with strangers and wish each other well. There, lying in the snow by the fountain, was a little girl's thin, lifeless body, surrounded by spent matches. For the little matchgirl had left it there when she had gone away with her grandmother. She had no need of it in the place where they were going: a place without cold, nor hunger, nor pain – just happiness.

ST CHRISTOPHER

a European legend

Once there was a man called Christopher, who saw God all around him in the world and loved the Lord very much. As Christopher pulled endless weeds out of his vegetable patch he would pray, "Thank you, God, for sending the sunshine to make crops grow." As Christopher hammered away at his leaky roof on stormy nights he would pray, "Thank you, God, for sending the rain to water the land and fill the rivers and seas."

Christopher felt that because God did so much for him, he wanted to spend his life doing things for God in return. He knew that holy men like monks worked for God by spending their lives shut away in monasteries, praying. But Christopher didn't think that would suit him at all. He was very tall and very strong, and was much better at *doing* things than keeping still and silent.

Christopher's little wooden house lay by a wide, churning river, and it was while he was watching the raging waters one day that he had an idea. There was no bridge across the river and no ferryman either. But Christopher was sure that he could wade through the river carrying the travellers on his shoulders. Christopher knew that each

trip would be ice-cold, exhausting and dangerous, but he was
determined to work for God by helping other people.

And that's exactly what he did. No
matter what time of day or night
travellers arrived at his hut,
Christopher stopped whatever
he was doing, stripped off his
shirt, and plunged into the
freezing river. Time and time
again Christopher carried
men, women and children
across to the other side – and
often back again, too – and never
took a single penny from anyone for his
efforts.

One day, a little boy knocked on Christopher's door, all on his
own. "Will you carry me across, mister?" he asked.

"No trouble at all," smiled Christopher. He caught the child up
in his big, safe hands and tossed him high into the air a few times
until he was chuckling with delight. Then Christopher swung the
little boy onto his shoulders and strode out into the water, bellowing
a rousing song to drown out the scary rushing of the river.

Christopher was only waist-deep when he realised he was in
trouble. Somehow, the little boy had suddenly become heavier than
three fully grown men put together. And with every step deeper into
the swirling water, the child weighed more and more – heavier than
an ox . . . heavier than a load of bricks . . . heavier than his entire
house! Christopher sank into the riverbed under the immense burden,
and the waters came rushing around his chin. Still Christopher strode

on, but the waters came crashing over his face, filling his nose and mouth with liquid instead of air. Still he pressed forwards – even when the river rose above his eyes. His one desperate thought was to keep the child above water and get him safely to the far bank. Just when Christopher thought his lungs were about to explode and he would surely drown them both, he felt the steep uphill slope underfoot that led to the opposite bank. Christopher ploughed out of the river with his last drop of energy, lowered the little boy to the ground, and collapsed on all-fours in the sunshine.

"Thank you," came the child's soft voice, "for carrying God's son for a while and taking the weight of all the sins of the world onto your own shoulders."

Christopher's heart leapt for joy as he realised at last that the mysterious little boy was Jesus Christ himself. Gasping, he looked up – but the child had already vanished . . .

Many people today pray to St Christopher to look after them and help them when they are going on a journey. And now you know why he is always pictured wading through a river with a little boy on his shoulders.

THUMBELINA

retold from the original tale by Hans Christian Andersen

Once upon a time there was a woman who wanted more than anything in the world to have a child – but she didn't know where to get one. She went to see a witch about it and the witch gave her a special seed. The woman planted the seed in a flowerpot and it grew . . . and grew . . . and grew . . . into a bud that looked very much like the bud of a tulip. "What a beautiful flower!" the woman murmured one day, and she leant over and kissed the closed petals. POP! the bud exploded into an open flower, and there sitting in the middle of it was a tiny little girl, no bigger than the woman's thumb. The woman was overjoyed with her beautiful daughter and named her Thumbelina. The woman thought that her tiny daughter was utterly delightful and looked after her tenderly. But one night, a big, fat toad came hopping through a broken pane of glass in the woman's window. *Hmmm,* thought the toad, as her bulging eyes caught sight of Thumbelina sleeping in half a walnut shell. *She would make a perfect wife for my son.* The toad picked up the dreaming little girl, bed and all, and hopped away to the marshy river where she lived. The toad swam out to where the water ran fast and deep and placed Thumbelina in her walnut shell on a broad, flat lilypad. *Now you can't run away,* the toad thought, and she swam off to break the good news to her son . . .

When Thumbelina woke up and saw that she was not only lost, but trapped too, she began to cry bitterly. The fish wiggled up to see what was causing all the tiny splashes and ripples, and they took pity on the sad, tiny girl. Quickly and silently, they nibbled through the lilypad's green stem and Thumbelina went floating off down the river.

Soon, she was far out of the toads' reach . . . and still the lilypad raft floated on. Thumbelina sailed past towns and was swept out into the countryside. Thumbelina liked it among the fields. It was sunny and peaceful, and a pretty white butterfly fluttered down to keep her company. Suddenly a large flying beetle dive-bombed the lilypad and wrapped his legs around Thumbelina's tiny waist. In a flash, Thumbelina found herself sitting on a twig with the beetle high up in a tree, watching her lilypad drift away without her.

Hundreds of the beetle's curious friends came crawling out of the bark to peer at what he had brought home. "Urgh! Look, it's only got two legs," the beetle children squealed.

"Where are its feelers?" some of the lady beetles murmured.

"Hasn't it got a slim bottom?" other lady beetles gasped in horror, admiring their own round shiny ones.

"It is rather ugly," the male beetles had to admit. "Let's get rid of it." And they flew down from the tree with Thumbelina and sat her on a daisy.

Poor Thumbelina felt very like crying. But just then she noticed a little hole in the earth below her that looked very like it was a type of doorway. She jumped down from the daisy and peered into the gloom. "Hello!" she cried. "Is anyone at home?"

After a few seconds, out popped a fieldmouse's head. She looked Thumbelina up and down, and tutted loudly. "Dear, dear!" the fieldmouse scolded. "You look exhausted and hungry. If you're as lost as you look, you're very welcome to stay here with me – in return for keeping my rooms nice and clean and tidy."

So all winter Thumbelina lived with the fieldmouse. Every day, she washed and swept and scoured and polished, and the fieldmouse was very kind to her. Although, truth to tell, Thumbelina found life rather boring. The fieldmouse wasn't at all skilled at making entertaining conversation and neither was her regular visitor, Mr Mole. Mr Mole came once every week in his fine black velvet overcoat. He didn't like to talk. He just enjoyed sitting and peering at Thumbelina through his little, short-sighted eyes, and listening to her sing.

The fieldmouse was delighted that her friend so liked Thumbelina. "I think he's falling in love with you," she whispered to Thumbelina excitedly. The fieldmouse was even more sure that she was right when Mr Mole invited them both to visit him in his splendid underground mansion.

"I have dug a tunnel from your house to mine," Mr Mole informed them, "so you may come and see me in comfort. Only please close your eyes when you are halfway down the passage, for I am afraid that a dead swallow is lying there."

Thumbelina wasn't at all revolted when she came across the dead bird on her first trip to Mr Mole's house. Instead, she felt pity for the poor thing, lying all stiff and still on the cold earth. While the fieldmouse ran on eagerly ahead, Thumbelina bent down and stroked the bird's feathers. "Goodbye, sweet swallow," she murmured, and she laid her head on the bird's soft breast. DUP! DUP! DUP! Thumbelina heard the swallow's heart beating – only very faintly, but Thumbelina knew that the bird was still just alive!

From then on, Thumbelina found as many excuses as possible to creep away from the fieldmouse and into the tunnel to care for the swallow. Over the weeks that followed, she placed leaves under the bird's head and plaited a coverlet of hay to keep it warm. She dripped drops of water into its weak throat and fed it tiny morsels of food – and gradually the swallow began to recover. By the time the weather had begun to grow warmer, the swallow was well enough to stand and hop about. On the first day of spring, the swallow was totally better – and extremely grateful for all Thumbelina's kindness. "One day, I will repay you," he twittered as he hopped up the passageway and soared off into the blue sky.

It was then that the fieldmouse announced to Thumbelina that she had arranged for her to be married to Mr Mole. "He is very wealthy and will take good care of you," the fieldmouse beamed.

But Thumbelina was horrified. "I cannot live my life underground!" she cried, and ran sobbing out into the fields. She held her hands up to the sunshine and looked all around at the flowers, and she felt as if her heart would break.

Just then, Thumbelina heard a familiar twittering above her head. She looked up and saw her friend the swallow swooping down towards her. "Come away with me," cried the swallow, "I know a place where you will be happy. I have seen it on my travels." Joyfully, Thumbelina jumped onto his soft, feathery back.

The swallow flew off with Thumbelina over villages and roads, lakes and forests, snow-capped mountains, to a land where the weather was always sunny, where the breeze was always warm, and where in every flower there lived a tiny person just like Thumbelina. Thumbelina was very happy in her new home. She even married a handsome prince who lived in a rosebud and who was extremely glad that she had never become Mrs Mole! Best of all, the swallow came to visit every year in September, and stayed with Thumbelina and her prince each winter long.

BABUSHKA

a Russian folk tale

There was great excitement in the village where Babushka lived. All the old lady's neighbours were out of doors, peering up at the wintry night sky, where the biggest star anyone had ever seen was shining down at them. "Where has it come from?" everyone gasped in astonishment. "What does it mean?"

Only Babushka stayed indoors, getting on with her housework as usual. "What a lot of fuss about a star!" she muttered to herself as she swept and dusted, scrubbed and mopped, polished and tidied. "I haven't got time to waste, I've got standards to keep up." Babushka's house was always spotless and in perfect order.

RAT-TAT-TAT! came a loud knocking at the door.

"Now who's that interrupting my work?" Babushka frowned. She hurried to the door, plumping up the cushions and tidying a vase of flowers on the way. To her astonishment, three foreign-looking men were standing on the doormat, wrapped in long, embroidered robes and swathed in turbans. Even more surprisingly, the camels they had been riding were tied to the gatepost and were snorting puffs of steam into the crisp, cold air.

"Good evening, Babushka," the first man greeted her. He held out his hand and it jingled with bangles of gold, while jewelled rings sparkled on his fingers. "We are travelling from a far distant country, and we need a place to rest for the night. Would you be kind enough to welcome us in?"

Babushka could clearly see that the men were rich and important. "Of course . . . I would be honoured," she spluttered red-faced, and she welcomed her guests into her little sitting room while she quickly untied her apron and smoothed down her hair.

"What brings you to these parts?" Babushka asked politely, as she bustled about lighting a fire.

"We are following the strange star that shines so brilliantly," the second man explained.

"Really?" smiled Babushka, as she went to bring three plates of bread and cheese and pickles from the kitchen.

"We believe that it will lead us to a new king – the king of all heaven and earth,"continued the third man.

"Well, fancy that!" remarked Babushka, scurrying to fetch three steaming mugs of hot chocolate.

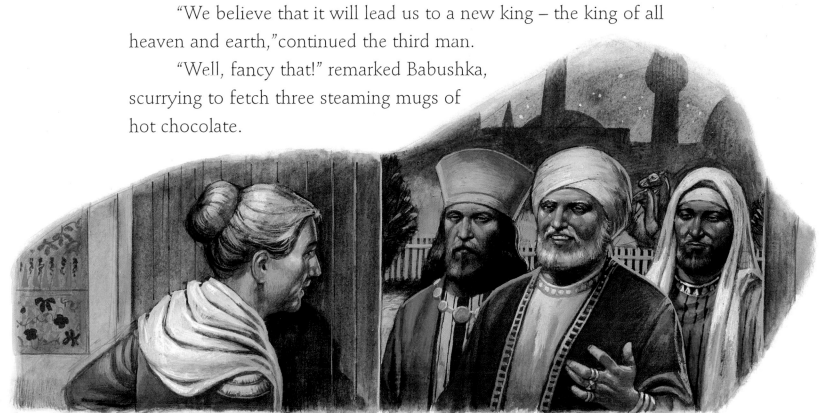

"Why don't you come with us, Babushka?" the first man urged. "We will be leaving tomorrow with our gifts of gold, frankincense and myrrh."

"Thank you, but I can't possibly come with you," said Babushka. "If I were to go away, who would air the beds and sweep the stairs and dust the shelves and scour the sink? Besides, I don't have anything that would be suitable as a gift for a king!"

"This king is newborn," the second man said kindly. "He is still only a tiny baby."

Babushka paused with a tray full of washing-up. "I had a baby boy once," she said in a whisper, "but he died."

The third man rose to his feet and put his hand gently on Babushka's arm. "Come with us," he said, softly. "Come with us to see the baby saviour of the world."

Babushka stood and thought for a while. Her eyes had a faraway look in them and there was a sad smile on her lips. "Maybe just this once . . ." she murmured to herself. Suddenly – CUCKOO! CUCKOO! CUCKOO! – the clock in the hall noisily broke the silence. "Oh dear, is that the time?" cried Babushka, springing back into action. "I must go and make up the guest beds!" and she sprang off up the stairs.

Next evening, the star shone brighter and higher in the sky than ever. "Are you sure you won't come with us, Babushka?" the three men pleaded as they mounted their camels ready to go.

"I'd love to, but I've got too much to do," the old lady blustered.

The three men waved sadly as they lurched away.

Babushka's heart was strangely heavy as she shut the door and went back inside her little cottage. She left her broom standing in the corner, the washing-up in the sink and the crumbs under the table, and she went and unlocked a cupboard in the corner of the sitting-room instead. Babushka sighed a deep sigh as she gazed at the shelves in front of her. They were stacked with toys of every size and colour. Babushka ran her fingers lovingly over them, wiping off a layer of dust. "My little son's toys would make a perfect present for the new baby king," she murmured.

It took Babushka all night to wash and dry and polish all the toys, until every single one was as good as new. As the sun came creeping through her window, she packed the toys in her shopping bag, put on her overcoat and headscarf, opened her cottage door and locked it behind her. Then she was off down the path.

Babushka walked and walked and walked – through villages and towns and cities. She lost all track of time, but she noticed one night that the star faded from the sky. A few days later, she came to the little town of Bethlehem. "Have you seen three men on camels, looking for a baby?" Babushka asked a local innkeeper.

"Why, yes," replied the innkeeper. "The three men were here all right. In fact, the baby was born in that very stable over there." He pointed to a dingy hut at the back of his inn. "The three men didn't stay long – just as well, really, because just after they'd gone, a group of shepherds came to see the baby too." The innkeeper laughed. "It would have been a bit crowded with everyone there at once! But I'm afraid you're a bit too late. After all the visitors had gone, the parents left with their baby last week."

Babushka looked from the empty stable to her full bag of toys. "I will go on searching until I find the baby," she decided. "I will give him my presents and ask him if he will be my king too." Then she turned on her heel and strode away determinedly . . .

Babushka is still wandering over the world today, looking for the baby king. No one notices her as she goes quietly from house to house, but whenever she sees a good girl or boy, she dips into her shopping bag and places a toy by their bed. It is only on one day every year that the children find Babushka's gifts – and that is Christmas Day, the birthday of Jesus, the baby in the stable.

RIP VAN WINKLE

an American legend

In a village in the foothills of the Catskill Mountains of America lived a man called Rip Van Winkle.

Everybody liked Rip. He was a generous, easy-going man who was always glad to lend a hand to his neighbours. In fact, Rip Van Winkle was always to be found doing anybody else's work except his own. And didn't his wife remind him about it all the time! Nag, nag, nag it was, all day long. "Rip, if you're not too busy varnishing Mrs Green's fence today, you can mend the holes in the shed. Instead of helping to burn the farmer's rubbish, you can feed the chickens and milk the cows. Then if you can stop yourself from building Arne Jacob's wall for him, there's our potatoes to dig up and the wagon to be washed down and the gutters to be cleared out and the yard to be swept and . . ." And so it was every day, on and on and on and on.

Every now and again, Rip Van Winkle whistled for his faithful dog Wolf, shouldered his gun, and strode away from his wife without a word. Off he would stroll up the mountainside, along the river and through the pine forests until his wife's screeching voice had

grown so faint that he could no longer hear it, and he was
surrounded only by the twittering of the birds, the rustling of the
trees in the breeze and the panting of his companion by his side. Rip
always knew there would be heck to pay when he got home. But a
day off in the peaceful sunshine was well worth it!

One day when Rip had disappeared on one of these rambles,
he was taking a rest under a shady tree, when he heard a voice calling
his name. "Rip Van Winkle! Rip Van Winkle! Rip Van Winkle!" came
the high, shrill cry.

Wolf's ears flattened against his skull and he gave a long, low
growl. Rip looked in the direction Wolf was snarling and there among
the long grass was a nodding green feather. The nodding green
feather was tucked into a bright red cap. The cap was on the head of
a bearded man no higher than his own boot, struggling under the
weight of a big beer barrel.

"Rip Van Winkle! Rip Van Winkle! Rip Van Winkle!" shouted
the dwarf, crossly. "Will you get yourself over here and give me a
hand with this barrel before it squashes me!"

Rip was so used to doing what he was told that he jumped up to help at once.

"That's better," wheezed the dwarf, as Rip took one end of the heavy barrel. "Now up we go!" Rip nearly tripped over as the dwarf stomped away up the mountain, pulling the barrel and Rip Van Winkle with him.

After at least an hour's tramping and much huffing and puffing, the dwarf led Rip Van Winkle straight behind a thundering waterfall, through a hidden door and into an enormous cavern.

Dwarfs were swarming everywhere. Some were dressed in aprons, pouring endless tankards of beer out of big kegs just like the one Rip was helping to carry. Others were playing nine pins, rolling smooth round black rocks at copper skittles and cheering loudly. Yet more dwarfs were drinking and clinking their tankards together, singing noisy songs.

"Pull up a chair," Rip's new friend invited him, lowering the barrel to the floor and passing him a tankard. "Help yourself to a drink. You must be gasping thirsty after that climb – I know I am!"

The stunned Rip Van Winkle did just that. "My, that's mighty powerful stuff!" he spluttered, as he swallowed down a huge gulp of the dwarf beer. "But whatever it is, it's very good!" He licked his lips and poured himself another tankardful. None of the dwarfs was taking a blind bit of notice of him, so Rip Van Winkle sat back and began to watch the nine pins competition. "Well, this is a most pleasant way to spend the afternoon," he thought, helping himself to another beer . . . and another . . . and another . . . and another. And before Rip Van Winkle even realised he was drunk, he had slumped forwards onto a huge flat rock and was snoring loudly.

When Rip woke up, the dwarfs were gone and the cavern was empty. "Come on, Wolf," he yawned, and they both stood up and stretched. "We'd better hurry back or we'll never hear the last of it." Through the little door they strode and out from behind the waterfall and off down the mountain. "Wait for it," he murmured to his dog as he climbed the porch steps to his house. "Any minute now, that wife of mine will start screeching fit to wake the dead." Rip put his hand on the doorknob and turned. He nearly walked smack-bang into the door as it failed to open. "Well, this needs a bit of oil," he murmured to himself. He rattled the knob and twisted it about. "Funny," Rip remarked, "I think it's locked. She never locks the door, never."

At that very moment, the front door opened and there stood a woman with an angry face. "Who are you?" the woman snapped.

"What are you up to, trying to get in my front door?" She was not his wife. In fact, Rip Van Winkle had never seen her before.

"Who are you?" gasped Rip. "What are you doing in my house?"

"*Your* house!" the woman scoffed. "I've lived here for over nineteen years!"

Rip Van Winkle backed off the porch and looked around him. He scratched his head and stared. The woman was right – it *wasn't* his house. Well, it looked similar to his house, but the curtains at the window were different. There were strange chairs on the verandah. The wagon in the yard was not his wagon.

"But – I – How –" stuttered Rip. "Where's Mrs Van Winkle?"

"Mrs Van Winkle?" the puzzled woman gawped. "She left here nearly twenty years ago, just after her husband wandered off and disappeared. Now, be off with you or I'll call the police!"

"*Twenty years!*" marvelled Rip Van Winkle, as he wandered away stroking his beard. His beard! Suddenly Rip realised that his beard hung down to his knees. The woman's words had to be true! He had been asleep for twenty years!

Rip Van Winkle's hands trembled with the shock as he reached down and patted the bemused Wolf comfortingly. Then his mouth began to curve upwards in a small smile. "Just imagine, Wolf," he murmured. "No more nagging – ever!" Rip Van Winkle turned and strode across the street, whistling a merry tune. Happily, the inn was in the same place it always had been – and when the townspeople heard his story, he never had to buy himself another pint of beer again.

THE GIRL WHO COULDN'T WALK
by Berlie Doherty

Once there was a girl who couldn't walk. Every day her father would carry her downstairs and put her in a chair by the window, and she would sit watching children playing in the lane on their way to school, running and skipping, chasing one another.

She loved to watch them. She was a happy child because it was her nature to be happy. She had never known what it would be like to walk, so she never complained. But her parents were not happy. Her mother complained all the time because she had been cursed with a child who could not walk. She wanted her daughter to be like all the other children. And her father complained because he had to carry her up and down stairs every day.

They brought doctors from all over the country to see what they could do for her, and the doctors would spend a long time examining her, and some would give her potions and some would give her exercises, some would stretch her and some would bend her, and they all ended up telling her parents the same thing: "I'm sorry, but your daughter will never walk."

"Send for another doctor," her mother would say. "Surely somebody can help her."

The girl would gaze out of her window and watch everything that was going on outside. She would wave to the children running down the lane, and she would watch the birds flying and the flowers unfolding and the clouds racing across the sky. She saw everything that was happening in the world outside her house, right up to the top slopes of the hill where the wild hares played. That was what she loved to look at most.

One day she noticed an old woman coming down the hill to the lane. The old woman was so bent that she had to use a stick, and her feet shuffled slowly along. It took her so long to come down the lane that the sun had moved from one side of the house to the other before she reached the gate, but the girl never took her eyes off her the whole time.

The old woman shuffled down the path and at last reached the

front door. She came into the room and stood in front of the girl, gazing at her and nodding her head, and then she turned to the parents.

"I can give her what she most wants," she told them.

"You!" scorned the girl's mother. "How can you cure her?"

"The best doctors in the world have tried, and all failed. What can you do?" the girl's father asked.

"Magic," said the old woman. "Magic."

The parents both turned their backs on her at once.

"You can each have one wish," the old woman said, "but you must keep it in your hearts. Once a wish is spoken the wish is broken. Remember that." And with that she went out of the house.

"What a stupid old woman," the mother said. "There's only one wish any of us can have, and that is for our daughter to walk. What can she do about that?"

As soon as she spoke there came such a rushing of wind that it seemed as if the whole house might fly up into the air. The doors and windows blew open, the carpets were lifted off the floor, the curtains

billowed out like puffs of smoke, and all the cups and plates rattled on the shelves like chattering teeth. And with the wind came a voice, shrieking through the open doors and windows like a great cry of pain.

"You have wasted your wish! You have wasted your wish! A wish spoken is a wish broken!"

The girl's mother clapped her hand to her mouth.

"What have I done!" she cried. "Now she'll never be like other children!" Her husband put his arm round her and comforted her.

They both turned to look at their daughter but she was gazing out of the window at the old woman, who had made her slow way to the end of the lane. She saw the old woman sinking down. She saw her crouch so she was almost touching the ground with her arms. She saw her hair turning brown and laughed with joy and reached out towards the window, as if for the first time she wanted to be on the other side of it.

The next day she was watching the hillside and saw what she was looking for. She said nothing to her parents. At last the old

woman reached the lane and started her slow journey towards the house, and still the girl said nothing. The door opened, and in the old woman came. She stood in front of the girl, gazing at her and nodding her head, and then she turned to the parents.

"Can you really make our daughter walk?" the girl's mother asked her.

"I told you what I can do," the old woman said.

"And can you really do it by magic?"

"Magic," the old woman nodded. "But you've had your wish. You've wasted it."

"I didn't believe in your magic. I didn't understand! Please can I try again?"

But the old woman turned away from the mother and spoke to her husband. "You still have your wish," she said. "Use it well."

"Can I have the same wish as my wife?" the man asked her.

"No." The old woman shook her head and shuffled out of the house and down the lane.

The man sat with his head in his hands.

"You have your wish!" his wife said. "You can use it to make our daughter better. Use it."

"How can I? There's only one wish I would make, and you've wasted it! What else can I ask for?"

"Say it in a different way!" his wife suggested. "Wish that...."

"Ssh!" her husband warned her. "A wish spoken is a wish broken, remember."

"But I'm only making suggestions," his wife said . "I can't have a wish anyway, so what I say doesn't count. Wish that…"

The husband put his hand across his wife's mouth. "Of course it counts! If it's spoken, it's spoken, isn't it! Leave it to me!"

He sat down again turning over in his head different ways of saying the same thing, and at last in despair he burst out, "How I wish you'd kept your mouth shut yesterday!"

As soon as he spoke there came a rushing of the wind, the blowing open of doors and windows, the lifting up of the carpets and the billowing out of the curtains, and the chattering of crockery on the shelves. And with the wind came a voice, shrieking through the open doors and windows like a great cry of pain.

"You have wasted your wish! You have wasted your wish! A wish spoken is a wish broken!"

But the girl heard nothing of this. She was gazing out of the window at the old woman making her slow way to the end of the lane. She watched her shrink down. She saw her crouch so she was almost touching the ground with her arms. She saw her hair turning brown and growing fast until it covered her body. She saw how her legs grew long and her arms grew short. The girl laughed with joy and reached out towards the window, straining with all her might to be out of the chair and on her feet.

All the next day she watched the hillside, and at last she saw what she was looking for. She said nothing to her parents. She watched as the old woman began to walk slowly down the lane, and still she said nothing. She watched her reach the gate and walk up the path to her house. The door opened, and in the old woman came. She stood in front of the girl, gazing at her and nodding her head, and then she turned to the parents.

"I'm sorry," the girl's father said. "I believed in your magic but I made the wrong wish. Please give me another chance."

"No," said the old woman. "There is no other chance." She turned back to the girl, who was watching every movement she made. "Now it is your turn to make a wish." And she went out of the house.

Anxiously the girl's mother and father circled round their daughter.

"Don't say a word!" her mother warned her. "You have to think it in your heart. A wish spoken is a wish broken, remember."

"And don't wish what your mother wished for," her father said. "Or it will be a wasted wish."

"I've already made my wish," the girl said.

Instantly there came a rushing of wind such as they had never heard before. The doors and windows blew open and the rugs were lifted off the floor. The curtains billowed out of the windows and all the plates and cups and saucers in the house rattled and chattered and shook. And with the wind came a voice, laughing through the open doors and windows like a great cry of joy.

"She wishes to be like me!"

"Like the old woman!" the girl's mother cried. "What a thing to wish for!"

"What have you done!" her father shouted.

But their daughter heard nothing of this. She was watching the old woman making her slow way up the lane. She reached out to the window as if she wanted to be on the other side of it. She saw how the old woman shrank, how she crouched to the ground, how her legs grew long and her arms grew short, how her hair turned brown and covered her body. The girl strained out of her chair as if she was trying to stand up. She saw how the old woman's ears grew long, how her eyes grew bright, how she straightened up, how she leapt forward. The girl stepped forward, one pace, two, three and with a bound she was away, out of the house, out of the path, out of the lane.

Her parents ran to the window, but all they could see, and all they would ever see, were two brown hares leaping and dancing to the very top of the hill.

A TALL STORY

an Indian folk tale

Five blind men were once sitting under a shady palm tree by the bank of the River Ganges in India, when they sensed that someone or something had silently crept up and joined them. "Who's there?" asked the first blind man. There was no reply, so he got to his feet and walked forwards with his arms outstretched. After a few steps, his hands hit something flat and rough and solid in front of him. "It's a wall!" he cried, triumphantly.

"Don't be stupid!" cried the second blind man, standing up. "How could someone have built a wall right under our noses without us hearing?" He, too, felt about in front of him. "Aha!" he said, delightedly, as he ran his hands down a hard, smooth, stick-like thing. "It's a spear, definitely a spear!"

At that, the third blind man got up to join them. "A wall and a spear!" he sneered. "Obviously, neither of you have any idea what this thing is." His fingers closed around something tatty and wiggly. "It's nothing more than a piece of old rope!" he laughed.

"How can you say that?" argued the fourth blind man, who had jumped up and joined in without anyone noticing. "I'm standing here with my arms wrapped around something so big that my fingers are barely touching together. It's a tree trunk, I'm telling you. A tree trunk!"

"I suppose I'll have to settle this," sniffed the fifth blind man, as he rose. He stuck out his hand confidently and grabbed hold of something long and swaying. "HELP!" he shouted. "It's a snake! It's a snake!"

Suddenly, whoops of laughter filled the air and the five blind men heard a little boy giggle, "You're ALL wrong! You're actually holding parts of an elephant – and you all look REALLY SILLY!"

At that, the first blind man stopped patting the elephant's side. The second blind man stopped stroking the elephant's tusk. The third blind man stopped holding the elephant's tail. The fourth blind man stopped hugging the elephant's leg. And the fifth blind man let go of the elephant's trunk. And from that moment on, the five blind men never argued again.

THE ADVENTURES OF SINBAD
THE SAILOR

a tale from The Arabian Nights

any moons ago, Sinbad the Sailor weighed anchor and sailed his merchant ship away from the ancient and magical city of Baghdad. The brave men voyaged into unknown waters for weeks, and by the time they spied land, they longed for the feel of solid ground underneath their feet. It was only a very small island that they saw – covered in sand, the grey of sea mists and with just two or three lone palm trees. Yet Sinbad and four others jumped into a little rowing boat and went ashore in case there might be coconuts or a pool of fresh water to top up their supplies.

Sinbad and his men were only halfway across the sandy island when a huge fountain of water suddenly jetted into the sky and the ground began to rock beneath their feet. As the sailors struggled to stay upright, they saw horror on the faces of their fellow crew members who had stayed on-board the ship. Their panic-stricken voices floated to them across the waves: "Whale!. . . It's a whale!" Then Sinbad realised they were not on an island at all, but on the back of a huge sea-creature who had been asleep for centuries. Sand had been blown there by the wind and a handful of palm tree seeds had put down shallow roots and sprouted. But at last the footsteps of Sinbad and his men had awakened the monster whale and now it was diving!

As the "island" began to sink into the sea, Sinbad watched his terrified crew hoist the sails of his ship and speed away. The ship disappeared from view just as the last patch of the whale's back vanished beneath the water, leaving the merchant and his men splashing and choking among the huge salt waves. One by one, Sinbad's men sank down after the whale into the depths, but Allah the merciful took pity on Sinbad and sent a barrel floating towards him on the waves. Sinbad collapsed exhausted over it as it bobbed like a cork on the swell.

The next thing Sinbad knew was waking up on a sandy beach, with the barrel beside him and gentle breakers lapping at his feet. He had no idea where he was. Jungle and mangrove swamps were on all sides. The only sign of habitation was a white dome a little way off and Sinbad set off at once towards it.

Sinbad found that the white dome wasn't a temple or a house. It was as smooth and curved underneath as it was on top, and there was no sign of a door. Sinbad sank down next to it, very frustrated. All at once, a huge shadow blotted out the sun and there was an ear-splitting "SQUAWK" as a giant eagle came wheeling down out of the sky. In a rush of wind, it settled its feathery bottom on top of the dome, smothering Sinbad underneath as if a soft mattress had been thrown on top of him. *"An egg!"* breathed Sinbad to himself, and after recovering from the shock, he thought up a brilliant plan to escape from the island. With much huffing and puffing, Sinbad wriggled himself into a position alongside the mammoth talons of the enormous bird. He unwound his long silk turban and tied himself as tightly as he could to the gigantic claw. Then Sinbad waited until in a rush of air, the eagle took off from her nest and soared into the sky, carrying the gasping merchant with it.

Sinbad shut his eyes tight against the glare of the sun as the eagle hovered higher and higher on the wind. On and on they flew before finally Sinbad's stomach gave a sickening lurch as the eagle swooped down to land in the middle of a rocky valley. Hurriedly, Sinbad untied himself and dashed away from the bird and its vicious beak. He hid behind a boulder for a while, trying to get his breath back, and as he took in his surroundings, his eyes opened wide with astonishment. Everywhere Sinbad looked, the earth was glittering with jewels! Diamonds and rubies and sapphires and emeralds carelessly covered the ground like pebbles on a beach. Sinbad stuffed his pockets and filled his boots until he couldn't carry even one jewel more. Then suddenly his face fell. How was he to get out of the rocky valley? Steep cliffs rose around him on all sides, impossible to climb. "What's the good of having pockets full of treasure," Sinbad pondered, "if all I can do with it is sit here and count it till I die?"

THWACK! A massive slice of raw meat fell from the sky and hit Sinbad on the head. "What in heaven – ?" began Sinbad. Then he realised what was happening. Back in the inns of Baghdad he had heard travellers' tales about a wonderful valley of jewels. Its cliffs were so sheer that no one was able to descend into the valley to reach the gleaming treasure. Instead, merchants threw down hunks of meat, in the hope that some of the jewels would stick to it. They then waited for the giant eagles who lived on the island to pick up the meat and carry it out of the valley. The merchants knew the eagles' favourite eyries, and they simply hid and waited and took the treasure.

Sinbad couldn't believe his good fortune. It was this very valley in which he found himself now!

Once again, Sinbad unwound his long, silk turban. This time he tied himself to the great big slice of meat that had fallen on his head. He was just in time. Almost immediately, an enormous eagle swooped down and snatched the meat – with Sinbad attached – and soared off into the air. Up flew the eagle, right out of the valley and away from the cliffs, alighting with a flutter on a rocky mountain ledge. While Sinbad untied his turban, a merchant popped up from behind a boulder to collect his booty. Of course, he was expecting to see jewels, not Sinbad, but when Sinbad offered to share his pockets of treasure, the merchant grinned a broad grin and promised to help him all he could . . .

By nightfall, Sinbad found himself in a crowded, prosperous port. After trading only a handful of his diamonds and rubies and sapphires and emeralds, he had enough money to buy not just one new ship, but an entire fleet – and to load them with cargoes of satins and silks and spices, too. And Sinbad sailed away across the even seas, hungry for more adventure . . .

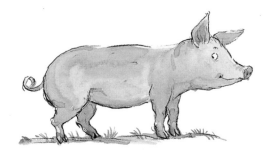

THE OLD WOMAN AND HER PIG
a traditional folk tale

L ong ago, an old woman found a bright, shining sixpence and went to market to buy a pig. She set off home with the pig trotting quite happily at her side. But when they were nearly there, they came to a stile and the pig wouldn't jump over it.

So the old woman went on a little further. She met a dog and said, "Dog! Dog! Bite pig. Pig won't jump over the stile, so I won't get home tonight." But the dog wouldn't.

So the old woman went on a little further. She met a stick and said, "Stick! Stick! Beat dog. Dog won't bite pig, and pig won't jump over the stile, so I won't get home tonight." But the stick wouldn't.

So the old woman went on a little further. She met a fire and said, "Fire! Fire! Burn stick. Stick won't beat dog, dog won't bite pig, and pig won't jump over the stile, so I won't get home tonight." But the fire wouldn't.

So the old woman went on a little further. She met some water and said, "Water! Water! Put out fire. Fire won't burn stick, stick won't beat dog, dog won't bite pig, and pig won't jump over the

stile, so I won't get home tonight." But the water wouldn't.

So the old woman went on a little further. She met a horse and said, "Horse! Horse! Drink water. Water won't put out fire, fire won't burn stick, stick won't beat dog, dog won't bite pig, and pig won't jump over the stile, so I won't get home tonight." But the horse wouldn't.

So the old woman went on a little further. She met a rope and said, "Rope! Rope! Lasso horse. Horse won't drink water, water won't put out fire, fire won't burn stick, stick won't beat dog, dog won't bite pig, and pig won't jump over the stile, so I won't get home tonight." But the rope wouldn't.

So the old woman went on a little further. She met a rat and said, "Rat! Rat! Gnaw rope. Rope won't lasso horse, horse won't drink water, water won't put out fire, fire won't burn stick, stick won't beat dog, dog won't bite pig, and pig won't jump over the stile, so I won't get home tonight." But the rat wouldn't.

So the old woman went on a little further. She met a cat

and said, "Cat! Cat! Scare rat. Rat won't gnaw rope, rope won't lasso horse, horse won't drink water, water won't put out fire, fire won't burn stick, stick won't beat dog, dog won't bite pig, and pig won't jump over the stile, so I won't get home tonight."

"All right," said the cat, " – if you get me some milk."

The old woman was highly surprised and fetched a saucer of milk at once.

The cat scared the rat, so the rat gnawed the rope, so the rope lassoed the horse, so the horse drank the water, so the water put out the fire, so the fire burnt the stick, so the stick beat the dog, so the dog bit the pig, so the pig jumped over the stile – and that's how the old woman got home that night!

THE BRAVE TIN SOLDIER

retold from the original tale by Hans Christian Andersen

A little boy was once given a box of twenty-five tin soldiers as a gift. They wore smart uniforms and proudly shouldered their guns, and the little boy was very pleased with them. Only one of the tin soldiers wasn't quite perfect, for he had just one leg. He and his brothers had all been made from the same tin spoon, and there hadn't been quite enough metal to finish him off. Still, it was because he stood out as being special that the little boy put him to stand guard at the gates of the toy castle, instead of keeping him in the box with the others.

The tin soldier was very honoured to have been given an important duty, and he stood to attention, staring straight ahead. His gaze landed on a beautiful tiny doll whom the boy had placed in the open castle doorway. She was made of the very best plastic and wore a ballet dress of thin muslin, tied at the waist with a shiny blue ribbon. She held both her arms gracefully over her head and she balanced beautifully on one leg, for just like the tin soldier, she had one leg missing. (Well, in actual fact that wasn't the truth. The girl's other leg was extended out behind her because she was a dancer. But the tin soldier wasn't in a position to see it.) *That would be just the wife for me*, the tin soldier thought at least ten times every day. But the tin soldier dared not go and tell the girl of his love for her, for he was on duty.

One morning, the tin soldier was unexpectedly relieved of his post. A sudden breeze blew through the open window causing the curtains to flutter and knocking the soldier right off his feet and over the windowsill. Down he tumbled through the air, until he landed headfirst on the pavement.

The tin soldier didn't cry out for he was brave-hearted in the face of danger – not even when big drops of rain began to bombard him from above. *So this is what it feels like to be out on the battlefield,* the brave tin soldier thought.

Eventually the rain stopped falling and two keen-eyed boys came along and spotted the tin soldier among the puddles. The boys quickly folded some newspaper into a boat, popped the tin soldier in the middle, and set him afloat in the rainwater that rushed down the gutter at the side of the street.

They ran alongside the boat as it swirled along, cheering it on its way delightedly. The tin soldier was shaking with fear inside, but he didn't flinch or move a muscle – even when the rushing water carried his newspaper boat down a drain and into the darkness under the pavement.

Suddenly a huge water-rat appeared.

"Who goes there?" it demanded, twitching its whiskers and baring its long teeth.

At last, I face the enemy! thought the brave tin soldier. But before he could lower his gun and aim it, his newspaper boat was carried past the rat on the tide.

A glimmer of light appeared in the distance and the rushing of the water grew louder and louder. The tin soldier realised with horror that he was being swept towards a sudden drop where the drain water casaded in a waterfall into a canal below. Even worse, the churning waters were splashing over the sides of the newspaper boat and the bottom was growing soggy beneath the tin soldier's feet. "Steady! Steady! Hold the line!" the brave tin soldier told himself. Suddenly the bottom of the boat ripped and gave way. The tin soldier plunged into the deeps and the icy waters closed over his head.

Surely now I am done for! thought the tin soldier, as he sank downwards through the murky wetness. Then all at once, everything went black as a fish swallowed him. The tin soldier choked and spluttered as he was gulped down into the fish's gullet, then the waters drained away and he was left lying on his back, holding tightly onto his gun. Even though the tin soldier couldn't see in the darkness, he could just about breathe in the stinking, rotten air. *So this is what it's like to be a prisoner of war in a dungeon*, the brave tin soldier thought to himself. And to keep up his spirits, he concentrated hard

on the beautiful dancing girl he had left behind him at the castle.

The tin soldier lost track of time inside the fish, but eventually he was flung to and fro as the creature was caught on a hook and struggled to escape. Then everything went quiet and still for quite a while, until suddenly the fish was cut open. "I don't believe it!" came a voice "Here's the missing tin soldier," and a woman with a kind face reached in and pulled him out. She gave the brave tin soldier a shower under a running tap, carried him into the drawing room and set him back in his old position outside his very own castle.

The tin soldier puffed out his chest with pride. *The war is over. I am back where I belong,* he thought to himself. He stared straight ahead, and there was his love, his sweetheart, the beautiful little dancing girl. *Tomorrow, as soon as I am off duty, I will definitely ask her to marry me,* the tin soldier decided. But then he felt an icy wind around his ankles, and a breeze coming through the window once more swept him off his feet and into the air. This time he landed in the blazing flames of the open fire – but the brave tin soldier didn't mind, for the dancing girl was blown in too and landed at his side. "Be brave, my love!" cried the tin soldier, holding his gun on his shoulder, and the dancing girl burst into flames and was gone. Then the tin soldier himself began to melt . . . and the next day, when the woman with the kind face was raking over the ashes, she found a tiny tin heart that the fire had been unable to burn away.

Feathers, Fur and Fangs

PUSS IN BOOTS

retold from the original tale by Charles Perrault

A certain miller was so poor that when he died, all he left his three sons were his mill, his mule and a cat.

"Bagsy me the mill," said the eldest son.

"Bagsy me the mule," said the middle son.

"Oh, great!" said the youngest son. "I suppose I'm left with the cat then." (As you can tell, he wasn't very happy about it. But youngest children often start off with a bad deal in fairytales, so he should really have seen it coming.)

"Stop your moaning!" scolded the cat. "If you stick with me, I can guarantee that you'll be thanking your dear old dad later. Now fetch me a large bag and leave me to get on with things. Oh – and get me a smart pair of boots made from the finest red leather, just like I've always wanted . . ."

The youngest son didn't argue. Firstly, the cat had never talked before, so he was speechless with shock. And secondly, he didn't have a better plan to suggest anyway. So he took what little money he had saved under the mattress and did exactly what the cat had told him . . .

As soon as Puss had finished purring with delight at how fine he looked in his smart boots of the finest red leather, he hurried along to a field and lay down quite still with his bag wide open beside him. After a while – hop! hop! hop! – along came a plump bunny. Pop! the silly rabbit jumped straight into the bag. Zip! Puss shut the bag. Whistling merrily, he took his catch to the palace and presented it to the king. "My master, the Marquis of Carabas, sends you this gift," Puss announced, bowing low.

"Give him my warmest thanks," the king announced, smiling graciously.

As soon as Puss was gone, the king turned to his chamberlain and whispered: "Whoever this Marquis is, he must be very rich and important to send his messengers in such smart boots!"

The next day the cat was back again – with a present of two partridges. And the day after that – with three pheasants. Every day for three months, Puss arrived at court with a gift for the king from his master, the Marquis of Carabas. "What a thoughtful, kind-hearted man this Marquis of Carabas is!" the king exclaimed as his royal pantry filled up with delicious game.

One day, Puss learned that the king was going to take a drive along the river with his beautiful daughter. "Right, you're going for a swim!" the cat commanded the miller's youngest son.

"But – but – I don't have any swimming trunks!" the Marquis of Carabas protested, but Puss was already dragging him along to a certain spot on the riverbank. Before he knew it, the cat had taken away all his clothes and he was swimming around obediently among the waterweed.

Just then, the royal carriage came trundling by. "Help! Help!" shouted Puss, running out onto the road and flagging it down. "The Marquis of Carabas is drowning!"

The princess squealed with fright as she peered out of the carriage and saw a man splashing about in the water. At once, the king ordered his guards into the river to pull him out.

"Your majesty," purred the cat, as the soldiers began trying to give the startled miller's son the kiss of life. "As if it wasn't bad enough that the Marquis of Carabas has nearly drowned, while he was in the water, robbers have stolen all his clothes!"

The king tut-tutted and sent his chamberlain galloping back to the palace to bring a selection of his very own robes for the Marquis to wear. Soon the miller's son was looking exceedingly handsome in the king's best suit, and the princess was blushing a deep pink. "It's the very least I can do in return for all the kind gifts you have been sending me!" the king said earnestly. The miller's son had no idea what the king was talking about, but he thought it best just to nod and smile all the same. "You will come and ride with us a while, won't you?" insisted the king, and the miller's son was ushered up into the royal carriage to sit next to the princess.

Puss was highly excited that his

scheme was working, and he ran ahead down the road. By and by, he came to a hayfield of mowers, and he said, "Good people, if you don't tell the king that this field belongs to the Marquis of Carabas, I'll make you all into cat food."

It wasn't long before the royal carriage passed by and, sure enough, the king leaned out of the window and asked, "Who does this land belong to?"

"It b-b-b-belongs to the M-m-m-arquis of C-c-c-arabas," the terrified mowers stuttered.

"You have a fine estate," the king beamed at the miller's youngest son, and the so-called Marquis nodded and smiled.

Soon the royal carriage came to a cornfield of harvesters. The miller's youngest son was just as surprised as the king to learn from the harvesters that the cornfield belonged to him, too! A little further down the road, and a group of dairymaids insisted that their cows belonged to the Marquis of Carabas.

"My!" the king grinned. "What splendid lands you have!" And the princess's cheeks turned quite rosy with pleasure.

While the royal carriage rolled along, Puss was a long way down the road at a fearful ogre's castle. It was the ogre who owned all the land that Puss had been giving to the Marquis of Carabas (though luckily, the ogre didn't know about that!). "Mr Ogre," began Puss politely. "I have come to pay my respects to you because I have heard that you have remarkable powers. Is it true that you can turn yourself from a big, hulking ogre into a tiny, sneaky mouse?"

"Easy-peasy!" growled the ogre. He disappeared before Puss's very eyes and suddenly there was a mouse scurrying about on the floor. It took Puss only a few seconds to pounce and gobble him up, and that was the end of the ogre.

By the time the royal carriage pulled up outside the castle, Puss was waiting outside to greet it. "Welcome to the home of the Marquis of Carabas," Puss announced proudly. The cat ushered the highly surprised miller's youngest son and his stunned royal guests inside, where they found a delicious banquet the servants had prepared for them at Puss's instructions.

"My dear Marquis," beamed the king. "I am most impressed with your riches – er, I mean generosity. If there's anything I can do for you, just say the word."

The miller's son glanced at the princess, who hissed under her breath, "Go on! Ask him!"

So the Marquis of Carabas cleared his throat and said, "Actually, I'd quite like to marry your daughter!" and the king roared with happy laughter.

The couple were married that very day, and the miller's youngest son lived as the rich and prosperous Marquis of Carabas for the rest of his life. So his story has a happy ending after all. (And that's what happens in fairytales, so he should really have seen it coming.) As for Puss – well, he lived happily at the castle too. There were plenty of mice to catch, and that's all he needed to be content – as well as his smart boots of the finest red leather, of course!

THE WONDERFUL TAR BABY

retold from the original tale by Uncle Remus

B rer Fox was doing what he usually did – trying to catch Brer Rabbit. But he'd be danged if this time he didn't catch that pesky varmint once and for all! Brer Fox mixed up a big pot of sticky tar and pulled and patted it into the shape of a baby. Then he lolloped up the road, set the tar baby sitting in the dust, and went to lay low in the ditch.

By and by, Brer Rabbit came bouncing down the road. "Good morning," he greeted the tar baby, "nice day, ain't it?"

But the tar baby didn't utter a word.

"I SAYS," shouted Brer Rabbit, just in case the tar baby hadn't cleaned his ears recently, "GOOD MORNING! NICE DAY, AIN'T IT?"

The tar baby just stared straight ahead.

"Ain't you got no manners?" Brer Rabbit asked, crossly.

Still the tar baby stayed silent.

By this time, Brer Rabbit was hopping from foot to foot, madder than a snake in a wasps' nest. "You'd better speak to me civil-like or else!" he hollered.

But the tar baby simply ignored Brer Rabbit.

"Well I guess you've done gone and asked for this!" Brer Rabbit shrieked. BLIP! he thumped the tar baby straight in the mouth – and his fist was stuck fast to the tar baby's face. "You let me go!" Brer Rabbit yelled. "Let me go – or I'll let you have another!" BLAM! Brer Rabbit socked the tar baby again and his other fist was glued tight to the tar baby's head. "I've warned you!" bellowed Brer Rabbit. SMACK! he kicked the tar baby and was left hopping around on one leg. "Don't make me do this!" Brer Rabbit shouted. WALLOP! another kick and the tar baby was holding him off the ground. "Right, you've really had it now!" Brer Rabbit screamed. THUNK! he head-butted the tar baby and found himself stuck eye-to-eye with the cheeky critter.

All this time, Brer Fox had been holding on to so much laughter he thought he was going to burst. Now he leapt out of his hiding place and howled, "My, oh my, Brer Rabbit! What type of mess have you got yourself into this time?"

"I suppose you're gonna have yourself a tasty barbecued bunny for supper this evening," Brer Rabbit admitted.

"Yep! You said it," grinned Brer Fox, licking his lips.

"Well I'm glad you're going to dress me up with some sauce and warm me over your fire," Brer Rabbit smiled. "I'd much rather you did that than throw me in that

briar patch over there."

Hang on a minute, thought Brer Fox, and his face fell. *That no-good rabbit seems quite pleased about being roasted!* "I've changed my mind," Brer Fox said out loud. "I'm gonna hang you instead."

"Ain't I glad it's good ol' hangin' and not being thrown in the briar patch!" sighed Brer Rabbit.

Brer Fox frowned. "I mean, I'm going to drown you!" he snarled.

"Fine, fine . . ." smiled Brer Rabbit gaily. "Dip me in the water and at least I'll die clean. Just don't throw me in that there briar patch, that's all!"

At that, Brer Fox was sure that the very worst thing he could do to Brer Rabbit was to hurl him into the briar patch. He grabbed him round the waist and pulled him hard and – SHLUP! – Brer Rabbit came unstuck from the tar baby. Brer Fox spun round and round and round and – WHEEEEEEEE! – Brer Rabbit went sailing high into the air and came down – DONK! – into the briar patch.

Brer Fox began to smile contentedly. "I've bested that bunny once and for all!" he chuckled, as he wiped his hands.

A high-pitched giggle came from the far side of the briar patch, and when Brer Fox squinted into the sunshine, he could just see Brer Rabbit hopping away into the distance. "I was born and bred in a briar patch, Brer Fox!" he was singing. "Hee hee! Born and bred in a briar patch!"

Brer Fox boiled with rage and thumped the very first thing that came to hand. And you know what that was, don't you?

THE BIG-WIDE-MOUTHED TOAD-FROG

by Patrick Ryan

One fine day long ago when birds did talk and beasts did sing and grasshoppers did spit tobacco, two young ones named Jack and Mary went out for a walk.

Jack and Mary walked for the longest time. They walked further than you could tell me and further than I could tell you. They walked up over hills and mountains and down through the dark green woods. And as they walked, they talked.

"Ah now Jack," says Mary. "Wouldn't it be good if we should catch a creature and keep it as a pet?"

"Ah now, Mary," says Jack. "It would be good. But what creature shall we catch?"

"One not very big," declared Mary

"Nor very small," declared Jack.

"One not very tame," cried Mary.

"Yet not very wild," cried Jack.

"Well, there's only one thing to do," said Mary.

"And what is that?" asked Jack.

"Set a trip-trap," Mary said, "to catch a creature to be our pet. And I know just how to do that."

So Mary showed Jack how to set a trip-trap. Twelve sticks they gathered from the green willow tree, long and strong and narrow as could be. Mary gathered six sticks and Jack a half-a-dozen more, and they wove together the first four. The next four sticks round the first ones were bound, and the last four tied the trigger for the trip-trap down.

Then Jack went home, and so did Mary. They let the trip-trap sit for all the night. Come the morning light the two friends ran, over hill and mountain, into the dark green wood, to see what creature the trip-trap did trap.

And lo and behold the creature it held was not very big nor yet very small, neither tame nor wild was it. It was round and wet and slimy and green, with tiny eyes and great hind legs, and the widest big-wide mouth that ever was seen.

"Look!" said Mary.

"Look!" said Jack.

"Our trip-trap has trapped a round, wet, slimy, green BIG-WIDE-MOUTHED TOAD-FROG!"

And so it had.

And Jack and Mary lifted the trap, and the BIG-WIDE-MOUTHED TOAD-FROG jumped and skipped and hopped right out of that.

"HELLO (gulp) Hello! (gulp) Hello!" shouted the Big Wide-Mouthed Toad-Frog. "WHAT ARE YOU AND WHAT DO YOU EAT?"

"How-do," said Mary. "I'm a

little girl named Mary. And I like to eat nuts and berries and apples and cherries and hominy and corn pone and succotash and sandwiches of cheese and fish and chips and ice cream and cake."

"(Gulp) OOOOO…! (gulp) AAAAAHH! (gulp) A-MAZ-ING!" said the Big-Wide-Mouthed Toad-Frog.

"Well-now," said Jack. "I'm a little boy named Jack. And I do like to eat grits and johnny cake and cracker jack and apple-y pie and peach-y cobbler and buttermilk biscuits and sausages and rashers and chips and peas and spinach and lettuce and carrots and candy-sweets."

"(Gulp) OOOOO…! (gulp) AAAAAHH! (Gulp) A-MAZ-ING!" said the Big-Wide-Mouthed Toad-Frog. "WELL, (gulp) I MUST BE OFF (gulp) AND AWAY! (gulp)."

And before Jack and Mary could catch the Big-Wide-Mouthed Toad-Frog for to keep him as a pet, he was up and away with a hop, a skip and a jump, for the Big-Wide-Mouthed Toad-Frog he wanted to see the Big-Wide-World.

Now the very first strange creature that the Big-Wide-Mouthed Toad-Frog did meet in his travels round the Big-Wide-World was a Big-Old-Brown-Fat Monster with Branches growing out of the side of her head.

"(Gulp) HELLO! (gulp) HELLO! (gulp) HELLO!" shouted the Big-Wide-Mouthed Toad-Frog. "WHAT ARE YOU AND WHAT DO YOU EAT?"

And the monster she Moo-ed and she Moo-ed and she Moo-ed. "I am a cow," she said. "And I like to eat thistles the colour of bright blue, and grasses and four-leaf clovers, too."

"(Gulp) OOOOO…! (gulp) AAAAAHH! (gulp) A-MAZ-ING!"

shouted the Big-Wide-Mouthed Toad-Frog.

And he hopped and skipped and jumped his way on through the Big-Wide-World.

And the very next wondrous strange creature that the Big-Wide-Mouthed Toad-Frog did meet in his travels round the Big-Wide-World was a Funny Little Thing that hung upside down and had Two Heads.

"(Gulp) HELLO! (gulp) HELLO! (gulp) HELLO!" shouted the Big-Wide-Mouthed Toad-Frog. "WHAT ARE YOU AND WHAT DO YOU EAT?"

"Ho-hum," yawned the creature. Hum-ho. I'm an opossum." "Ho-hum," yawned the baby opossum in his mama's pouch.

"Hum-ho, Me too."

"We like to eat berries and cherries and roots and twigs," they replied.

"(Gulp) OOOOO…! (gulp) AAAAAHH! (gulp) A-MAZ-ING!" shouted the Big-Wide-Mouthed Toad-Frog.

And he hopped and skipped and jumped his way on through the Big-Wide-World.

So the next Odd Beast that he saw was as Big as a Mountain and covered with a Fur Rug.

"(Gulp) HELLO! (gulp) HELLO! (gulp) HELLO!" shouted the Big-Wide-Mouthed Toad-Frog. "WHAT ARE YOU AND WHAT DO YOU EAT?"

"Grrrr!" growled the beast. "I'm a big brown bear. And I love to eat honey and fish and more fish and more honey."

"Gulp OOOOO…! (gulp) AAAAAHH! (gulp) A-MAZ-ING!" shouted the Big-Wide-Mouthed Toad-Frog.

And he hopped and skipped and jumped his way on through the Big-Wide-World.

Well, the next Queer Creature the Big-Wide-Mouthed Toad-Frog did meet in his journey across the Big-Wide-World was a Scary-Looking-Fellow with a Bushy-Stripy Tail and a Black Mask round his eyes – just like a robber bandit!

"(Gulp) HELLO! (gulp) HELLO! (gulp) HELLO!" shouted the Big-Wide-Mouthed Toad-Frog. "WHAT ARE YOU AND WHAT DO YOU EAT?"

And the fellow told him, "I'm a raccoon. I love to eat GARBAGE, RUBBISH and TRASH, the smellier the better!"

"(Gulp) OOOOO…! (gulp) AAAAAHH! (gulp) DIS-GUSTING!" shouted the Big-Wide-Mouthed Toad-Frog. And he hopped and skipped and jumped his way on through the Big-Wide-World.

Now the last monstrous beast the Big-Wide-Mouthed Toad-Frog did spy on his travels was a Long Green Log with a Great Big Smile who rolled and slithered along on his belly.

"(Gulp) HELLO! (gulp) HELLO! (gulp) HELLO!" shouted the Big-Wide-Mouthed Toad-Frog. "WHAT ARE YOU AND WHAT DO YOU EAT?"

And the smiling Log smiled a Great-Big-Wide-Mouthed Smile and he said, "Heh heh heh. I'm an alligator! And I just LOVE to eat BIG-WIDE-MOUTHED TOAD-FROGS!" said the alligator. "Have YOU seen any BIG-WIDE-MOUTHED TOAD-FROGS about?"

And the Big-Wide-Mouthed Toad-Frog's eyes got VERY VERY BIG and his Big-Wide-Mouth closed up and got very small and the Big-Wide-Mouthed Toad-Frog said with a squeak, "Nope, I've not seen any such thing as a Big-Wide-Mouthed Toad-Frog ever, not at all round here, not ever in all my life!"

Then the Big-Wide-Mouthed Toad-Frog hopped and skipped and jumped his way all the way back to Jack and Mary's trip-trap, as fast as he could hop and skip and jump. And in that trip-trap he stayed most merrily, and lived there a most long time for his life, because the Big-Wide-Mouthed Toad-Frog had learned an ever so important lesson: that it sometimes pays to keep a BIG-WIDE MOUTH SHUT!

THE DRAGONS OF PEKING

a Chinese folk tale

Once there was a prince so poor that he only ruled over a handful of peasants who lived in a cluster of wooden huts among some dry, dusty fields. The sad little place was called Peking. However, the prince was good-hearted and determined and had grand dreams of building Peking into a splendid city. The first thing he did was to work hard with all the men, women and children in the village to build a high, solid wall with broad gates to keep out bandits.

The people were delighted. But little did they know that with all their digging and clearing and carrying and building they'd disturbed two dragons who'd been asleep in an underground cave for thousands of years. And you can imagine how grumpy the dragons felt when they were woken from their lovely long nap! "Who does this prince think he is," the first dragon growled, "getting his people to come banging around our cave like that!"

"Let's teach them all a lesson," the second dragon snorted.

That night, the two dragons wove a spell that turned themselves into an old man and an old woman. Using magic, they

crept past the royal
guards and through several locked
gates and doors, and stole into the very room where the prince lay,
snoring soundly. The wrinkled couple asked, "O wise and gracious
lord, we have come to ask your permission to leave your city of
Peking and to take two baskets of water with us."

The prince stirred slightly in his sleep and murmured, "Why, of
course you may!"

The old man and woman hurried off to the river excitedly. It
was a narrow, muddy sort of river, but it was Peking's main source of
water. They dipped their baskets into the stream, and in only a
matter of minutes, the river dwindled to a trickle, then dried up
completely. For the disguised dragons' water baskets weren't normal

water baskets. They were enchanted water baskets that could never be filled, even if an entire ocean was to be poured into them. Next, the old man and woman took their water baskets (which were no heavier than before) off to the village spring. Soon, where there had once been a bubbling gush of water, there was just a muddy puddle. Then the old man and woman visited every house in the village, draining all the people's water baskets of every last drop. Finally, the bent-over pair hobbled off with their water baskets down the road that led out of Peking.

By the time the sun rose, the wicked old couple were far, far away. Shouts of horror rose up from all over Peking as the people woke up and discovered there was no water. Before long, there was a clamouring crowd outside the prince's house. "What shall we do?" they shouted. "Our lips are parched. We can't boil any rice for breakfast. Our crops are drying and withering in the sun before our very eyes!"

The prince wrinkled up his nose as a stinky smell wafted underneath his nostrils. "Oh dear," he sighed, "and none of you has been able to have a bath this morning, have you?"

The people shuffled about and looked down, red-faced.

Then suddenly the prince remembered his dream about the two old people and their water baskets. Being a wise person who believed in magic, he was very suspicious and dashed off to see his faithful old advisor straight away. The faithful old advisor said, "Aha!" and smiled a knowing smile, and waggled his finger a lot, and took the prince straight off to the dragons' cave outside the city. When the faithful old advisor saw the cave was empty, he said "Well, there you are then."

"Well, there I am – what?" said the prince, rather frustrated.

"My father was told about this cave by his father, who was told by his father, who was told by his father, who was –"

"Yes, yes!" cried the prince impatiently. "Get on with it!"

"The two dragons who were asleep here obviously weren't very impressed with your plans to improve the city. They've taken your water and gone!"

At once the prince called for his spear and his horse, and was gone down the road in a cloud of dust. There were many travellers on the road that morning, but the prince glanced at them all briefly and thundered past without stopping. At last, after hours of hard riding, he recognised the old couple from his dream and reined in his panting horse. "I gave my permission for an old man and woman to take my water," the prince yelled, "not the two dragons that you two really are!" He plunged his spear into each of their baskets and water immediately began to gush out in a cascading torrent. With a spine-chilling roar, the old couple began to change back into dragons before the prince's horrified eyes. But before the fire-breathing creatures could pounce on him, they were swept off in one direction by the swirling waters, while the prince on his horse was carried off in the other. All the surrounding countryside was submerged into a vast sea, and the prince's horse scrambled onto a jutting crag that poked up out of the water. It had once been the tip-top of a gigantic mountain.

"Now what am I to do?" frowned the soaking prince.

"I shall pray to Heaven for help," came a voice. The prince looked round in surprise and saw that it came from a Buddhist monk, who had been sitting there so silent and still that he hadn't even noticed him. The monk shut his eyes and bowed his head . . . and as he prayed – to the prince's enormous relief – the waters vanished. The prince thanked the Buddhist monk earnestly and began galloping back to Peking.

As soon as the prince neared the high, solid wall he had built around his city, his people came pouring out of the gates with happy faces. "You'll never believe it!" they cried. "All our water has come back. But best of all, a brand new fountain has sprung up! It has swelled the river with water more sweet and crystal clear than any we have ever seen!"

Thanks to the magical fountain, the land around Peking stopped being dry and dusty and became green and beautiful. The prince fulfilled his plans of making the city one of the most splendid in the world, and – as far as the people know – the dragons have never come back.

THE HARE AND THE TORTOISE

retold from the original fable by Aesop

The day that Tortoise challenged Hare to a race, all the animals laughed so hard that their tummies ached. But Tortoise was fed-up with Hare whizzing round him all the time, teasing him about how slow he was. *I'll show that Hare, if it's the last thing I do!* Tortoise promised himself.

Hare thought that Tortoise's little joke was extremely funny. For that's all Hare thought it was – a joke. Hare never expected that Tortoise would actually go through with his mad idea. So his eyes nearly popped out of his head when he arrived at the starting line to see Tortoise already there, limbering up in a very slow, stiff, creaky sort of way.

"Be careful there, old chap!" Hare worried, as he realised his friend was serious. "You don't want to do yourself an injury."

"Don't worry about me," replied Tortoise. "You should be working out how you're going to beat me. Ha! You won't see me for dust!"

A huge crowd of animals had gathered to watch the race and they all cheered and clapped and jumped up and down at Tortoise's bold remark.

Suddenly, Hare started to feel rather annoyed. "All right then. If that's the way you want it!" he snapped. "I was going to give you a headstart, but obviously you won't be wanting one."

"No need," breezed Tortoise, although his little heart was pumping inside his shell. "First one to the windmill's the winner."

Hare peered into the distance. The windmill was three fields away. He could get there in under a minute without even losing his breath. But surely it would take Tortoise all day to reach it!

"Three! Twit-Two! One!" cried Barn-Owl, and Tortoise lifted one leg over the starting line amid thunderous applause.

The stunned Hare watched in amazement as Tortoise began to crawl slowly away. *Well, you have to hand it to Tortoise!* Hare thought, seeing the funny side of things again. *He's certainly got a good sense of humour and a lot of guts!*

Hare sat down next to the starting line under a shady tree. It was a beautiful sunny day and it was very pleasant to sit there in the dappled light, watching Tortoise amble peacefully into the field. Hare's eyes shut and his head drooped before he even realised he was sleepy . . .

Meanwhile, Tortoise was remembering what his dear old mum had told him as a child: *Slow and steady does it, son. Slow and steady does it.* And Tortoise kept on going and didn't give up . . .

Hare didn't wake up until the night air was so cold that it was freezing his whiskers. *Where am I?* he thought. And then suddenly he remembered the race. Hare leapt to his feet and squinted into the moonlight, but there was no sign of Tortoise. All at once, he heard a faint sound of cheering coming from a long way off, and he saw tiny dark figures jumping up and down around the windmill. "Surely not!" Hare gasped, and shot off over the fields like an arrow. He arrived at the windmill just in time to see all the animals hoisting Tortoise – the champion! – on their shoulders. And of course, after that, Hare never ever teased his friend about being slow again.

MONSTER FILM

by Russell Hoban

There was a little family of monsters and their name was Scalybum: Mum and Dad and Robert. They lived far away in the mountains. They had a monster TV and when there was nothing on TV they hired videos. They watched *Jumboola* and *The Return of Jumboola*. They watched *Bride of Jumboola*, *Jumboola Strikes Back* and *Bride of Jumboola's Vengeance*.

Dad never missed a monster film but he thought most of them were not very good. "They do not even use real monsters," he said. "Those are only little dolls."

One evening after they had watched *Jumboola Strikes Back Again* for the ninth time Dad said, "Robert could do better than that with our camcorder."

"How would I do it?" said Robert.

"You think up a little story," said Dad, "and Mum and I will help you with the rest of it."

"Make it a love story," said Mum.

"But there has got to be action," said Dad. "It is no good just having your monsters sitting around kissing and cuddling."

Robert thought about it and the next day he said, "I have got a sort of idea for a film."

"Tell us," said Mum.

"There is this beautiful girl," said Robert.

"A people girl or a monster girl?" said Dad.

"A monster girl," said Robert. "She sings a lot."

"What is her name?" said Mum.

"I do not know," said Robert.

"I think Melodina is a very pretty name," said Mum. "Did you have anyone in mind for the part?"

"I thought maybe you could do it," said Robert.

"I will sing but I will not dance," said Mum. "I draw the line at dancing."

"No dancing," said Robert. "Melodina loves to wander in the mountains picking flowers and singing. There is a monster composer spending a few weeks in the mountains."

"Rodolfo would be a good name for him," said Dad.

"Rodolfo is in the mountains because nobody liked the last thing he composed," said Robert. "His doctor told him he should get away from everything and have a good rest. One day Rodolfo hears Melodina singing. He gets all excited and he follows the sound, leaping from rock to rock. Then he sees her and he falls in love with her."

"That is nice," said Mum, "I like that."

"I hope there is going to be some action," said Dad.

"There is action coming," said Robert. "Melodina does not know that Rodolfo has seen her and he is too shy to say hello. He follows her around and he writes music."

"He is inspired," said Mum. "Melodina inspires him."

"Right," said Robert. "He is writing Melodina music."

"A symphony," said Mum. "His Melodina symphony."

"We hear that music when he looks at Melodina," said Dad.

"But now there is other music," said Robert. "Here come some people vans. On the sides of the vans it says SCUM."

"A rock group?" said Dad.

"Heavy metal," said Robert. "They are in the mountains to make a video."

"Under their music we can still hear the Melodina symphony music," said Dad. "That is how they do it in films."

"Melodina is still picking flowers and singing," said Robert, "and the SCUM lead singer and guitarist hears her."

"Oh, dear," said Mum.

"He follows the sound of her voice and he sees her," said Robert. "He tells her he can take her away from all this and make her rich and famous."

"Where is Rodolfo?" said Dad. "What is the matter with him?"

"He is busy writing his music," said Robert. "Melodina says no to the SCUM leader but he runs back to his van and gets a gun with one of those darts that put you to sleep."

"That man is no gentleman," said Mum.

"I saw this coming as soon as I heard the name of the group," said Dad.

"He wants to put Melodina on stage in a great big cage," said Robert.

"Melodina will never sing for him in a cage," said Mum.

"Melodina is running away up the mountain and the SCUM lead guitarist is running after her," said Robert. "Then he stops and he says, "If you will not sing for me you will not sing for anybody." The band starts playing as hard as they can and he tells his sound man to turn up the volume.

"I know what is coming," said Dad.

"On the mountains above Melodina," said Robert, "we can see some little rocks rolling down, then some bigger ones."

"Oh, no," said Mum.

"Rockslide," said Dad.

"Now it looks as if the whole top of the mountain is sliding down towards Melodina," said Robert. "But Rodolfo sees what is happening."

"Under the roar of the rockslide and the crashing of the SCUM music we hear the Melodina symphony music getting stronger," said Dad.

"Come on, Rodolfo!" said Mum.

"Here he comes," said Robert. "He throws down his notebook and he is leaping from rock to rock. He is trying to get to Melodina before the rockslide does."

"Go, Rodolfo!" said Dad.

"Save Melodina!" said Mum.

"Rodolfo grabs Melodina," said Robert. "He leaps to safety with her in his arms. The rockslide goes thundering down the mountain and the SCUM lead guitarist is standing in its path."

"I cannot look," said Mum.

"He brought it on himself," said Dad.

"But wait," said Dad. "Rodolfo has got a coil of rope over his shoulder. He was going to do a little mountain-climbing before this happened. He throws one end of the rope to the SCUM lead guitarist and saves him too."

Mum was crying. "You will play Rodolfo," she said to Dad.

"I will do my best," said Dad.

"Now the SCUM vans are moving out," said Robert. "They drive slowly down the mountain."

"Rodolfo takes Melodina in his arms," said Mum. "He tells her how she inspired him, he tells her how he loves her."

"And the Melodina symphony music comes up very strong for the ending," said Dad.

"Do you think my story will make a good film?" said Robert.

"I think it is wonderful," said Mum. "What will you call it?"

"Melodina Symphony is the only name for it," said Dad.

"Right," said Robert. "How do we do the people and the vans and all that?"

"We will use dolls for the people and models for the vans and the rest of the people gear," said Dad.

"It sounds like a lot of work," said Robert.

"It will be worth it," said Dad. "With this film I think we could break into the monster-film business."

Mum and Dad and Robert worked for months on the dolls and the models. Dad bought a book that told them how to make it look as if the dolls and the models were moving. It was very hard to do.

Then came the Melodina and Rodolfo part of the film. Robert worked the camcorder and Mum and Dad did the acting. They had a lot of trouble with the rockslide. They had to do it several times to get it right and it was hard work to carry the rocks back up the mountain each time.

Dad had to buy some new equipment for some of the things they had to do. Then he bought more books that told them how to do those things.

After they did all the voices and put all the parts of the film together Robert wrote the SCUM music and Mum wrote the Melodina symphony music. Then Robert played his music on his electric guitar and Mum played hers on the piano and they put the music on the film.

At last the film was done. Mum and Dad and Robert watched it over and over and Mum cried every time.

"I will send a copy of this to Megafright International," said Dad. "They are the people who make the best monster films. Maybe they will give us a lot of money for it. Maybe they will sign us up to make films for them."

Dad sent Melodina Symphony to Megafright International in Peopletown. It came back in two days. There was a letter with it:

Dear Mr Scalybum,

Your film is not very good. In fact it is pretty bad. The music is OK and

the human actors are all right but anybody can see that the rockslide is a fake and the monsters just do not look real enough.

> *Faithfully yours,*
> *J M Flatbrain*
> *President, Megafright International*

"Do not look real enough!" said Dad. "I think I had better have a word with Mr Flatbrain."

"I have heard that Peopletown is not a friendly place," said Mum.

"That is all right," said Dad, "because I do not feel very friendly just now."

"Robert and I will go with you," said Mum, "and I think we should all put on some helicopter repellent." When they had done that the Scalybums set out for Peopletown.

When Peopletown saw the Scalybums coming there were sirens, whistles, and public announcements. Buildings emptied as everyone tried to leave at once and there were traffic jams on all the roads. Swarms of helicopters came at them but the helicopter repellent repelled them.

"How can anyone live in a place like this?" said Dad as he brushed away missiles and fighter planes.

"I suppose they are used to it," said Mum.

The Scalybums tried to be as careful as they could but they kept getting their feet stuck in traffic jams. When they got them unstuck they could not help knocking over a few buildings. They also got tangled in all kinds of wires that pulled a lot of other things down.

"Mind where you step," said Mum.

"How do they expect me to see where I'm going if they keep squirting water in my face?" said Dad as he kicked some fire engines out of the way.

The people at Megafright International had not noticed the noise. They were still in their offices. Dad lifted the top off the building and said to the receptionist, "I'd like to see Mr Flatbrain, please."

"We do not need any actors today," said the receptionist without looking up. "Phone us next week."

"I am not an actor," said Dad.

"Oh, no?" said the receptionist.

"I am a monster," said Dad

"That is what they all say," said the receptionist. "Phone us next week."

"Look at me," said Dad. "This is not a costume. I am not an actor."

The receptionist looked at Dad and Mum and Robert. "Have a seat, please," she said. They all sat down on a nearby building. "What is your name?" she said.

"Scalybum," said Dad. "John Scalybum. This is my wife

Serafina and this is our son Robert."

"What do you want to see Mr Flatbrain about?" said the receptionist.

"Our film," said Dad. "Melodina Symphony."

The receptionist spoke to Mr Flatbrain on the telephone. Then she said to Dad, "He says to send it to him and he will look at it."

"I have done that," said Dad.

The receptionist spoke to Mr Flatbrain again. Then she said to Dad, "He wants to know if that is the one with the rockslide."

"That is the one," said Dad.

The receptionist spoke to Mr Flatbrain again. Then she said to Dad, "Mr Flatbrain says the monsters are just not real enough."

Dad reached into the office behind the receptionist and picked up Mr Flatbrain. "What about me?" he said. "Am I real enough?"

"Not really", said Mr Flatbrain. "You are pretty real but you will have to get a lot realer if you want to break into the monster business. Try again and let us see your next film."

"Not likely," said Dad. He put Mr Flatbrain down. "I think it is time to go home, he said to Mum and Robert. "I have had enough of this place."

Dad put the top back on the Megafright International building. Then Mum and Dad and Robert tidied up Peopletown as well as they could. Then they went home. When they got their feet up and settled down to watch TV they all felt better.

"Look," said Mum. "There we are on the *Six o'Clock News*. Why did I wear that hat. Nobody is wearing that kind of hat this year. I look awful."

"You look terrific," said Dad. "You always do. Do I look real to you?"

"You will always look real to me," said Mum, "and you will always be my Rodolfo."

"Our film was not a success," said Dad.

"It was fun though," said Robert. "I never really wanted to break into the monster business anyway. Can we watch *Jumboola* tonight?"

"Yes," said Mum and Dad. So they did.

THE ELEPHANT'S CHILD

retold from the original tale by Rudyard Kipling

There was once a time when the elephant had no trunk. All the elephant had for a nose was a blackish bulgy snout, which could sniffle and snuffle but couldn't pick anything up. And at this time there lived a very, very young elephant's child – so young that the world was still strange to him and he was finding out all about it by asking his family and friends a lot of questions. The elephant's child found out about things such as: where the sun slept (deep inside the lake); why his friend zebra had stripes (because he would have looked very silly with spots); and why ant-eaters ate ants (because they weren't called pigeon-eaters or turtle-eaters, were they?). But there were still a couple of things that the elephant's child didn't know: What did Mr Crocodile look like? And what did Mr Crocodile have for his dinner? And because the elephant's child had no more family or friends left to ask, he wandered away on his own to find out.

By and by the elephant's child reached the great grey-green, greasy Limpopo River, set all about with fever-trees. There he came across a lumpy log of wood lying in the water, blinking its yellow eyes and smiling a toothy grin.

"Excuse me," said the elephant's child, "can you tell me what Mr Crocodile looks like?"

"Well yes I can," said the lumpy log of wood. "I am Mr Crocodile and I look like this."

"Thank you very much," said the elephant's child. "I don't mean to be a bother and a nuisance, but can you also please tell me what Mr Crocodile has for his dinner?"

"Now that's a big secret," beamed Mr Crocodile. "Kneel down and bend close to me and I'll whisper it into your ear."

All excited, the elephant's child knelt down and bent close to Mr Crocodile.

SNAP! Mr Crocodile opened his long, razor-sharp jaws and clamped them firmly around the elephant's child's nose.

"Ow!" yelled the elephant's child. "Led go! You are hurtig be!"

But Mr Crocodile didn't let go. He held on tighter than ever and pulled and pulled and pulled.

Now the elephant's child liked swimming, but he didn't want to go into the water today, thank you very much. So he sat back on his wrinkled trousers and pulled and pulled and pulled.

Mr Crocodile thrashed with his wide, flat tail, sending water splashing everywhere. And he pulled and pulled and pulled.

And the elephant's child dug deep with his broad, round feet into the mud. And he pulled and pulled and pulled.

Just when the elephant's child thought that he was going to have to take a dip anyway, a friendly bi-coloured-python-rock-snake wriggled past and saw that he was having a bit of trouble. The friendly bi-coloured-python-rock-snake helpfully tied his head end around the elephant child's waist and looped his tail end around a handy nearby boulder, and pulled and pulled and pulled.

Suddenly the elephant's child's nose came free with a PLOP! that echoed all around the fever-trees up and down the great grey-green, greasy Limpopo River. "Thank you very much," the elephant's child said to the friendly bi-coloured-python-rock-snake, and he began to wrap his very sore nose in cool banana leaves. But the elephant's child didn't like the feel of what had happened to it. His nose felt longer and thinner and definitely – well, *stretched*. He sat in the mud looking dejected and touching it tenderly.

"That's a fine long trunk you've got there," said the friendly bi-coloured-python-rock-snake. "I'll bet you can pick things up with that and use it to shower yourself with water, and all sorts!"

"Really?" said the elephant's child, brightening up.

"I'd say that trunk is very useful and very handsome too," said the friendly bi-coloured-python-rock-snake. "I'll bet that when you go back home, all the other elephants will want one just like it." And so he wasn't surprised at all when, some weeks later, he saw a long line of elephants all queueing up on the banks of the great grey-green, greasy Limpopo River, set all about with fever-trees, to see Mr Crocodile and ask him what he had for dinner.

THE MOON IN THE POND

retold from the original tale by Uncle Remus

Every now and again Brer Fox and Brer Rabbit would shake hands and make peace for a while and, following their example, all the critters would forget their arguments and get along together just dandy. It had been like this for some weeks when Brer Rabbit ran into Brer Turtle and they got talking.

"It sure is peaceful around here now," sighed Brer Rabbit.

"Yep," nodded Brer Turtle, who was a man of few words.

"It sure is quiet," sighed Brer Rabbit.

"Yep," nodded Brer Turtle.

"Peaceful and quiet is good, but it ain't fun like in the old days, is it Brer Turtle?" asked Brer Rabbit.

"Nope," agreed Brer Turtle.

"I think that the folks round here could do with a dose of fun again," sighed Brer Rabbit.

"Yep," nodded Brer Turtle.

Brer Rabbit bounced to his feet with a chuckle. "Then I'm going to invite everyone to a little fishing frolic at the pond tomorrow night," he said. "I'll do all the talking as long as you back me up with your 'yep' and 'nope' now and then." And Brer Rabbit and Brer Turtle shook hands. Brer Rabbit loped off to do the inviting and Brer Turtle set out for the pond, so as he'd be sure to get there on time . . .

Sure enough, the following night, everyone was there at the pond. Brer Bear and Brer Wolf had brought their hooks and lines. Brer Turtle carried a pot of wriggling bait. Brer Fox brought his fishing net.

Miss Meadows and Miss Motts brought themselves, dressed up to the nines.

While Brer Turtle shook his pot at Miss Meadows and Miss Motts and made them squeal with delight, Brer Bear announced he was going to fish for mud-cats. Brer Wolf said he was going to fish for horneyheads. Brer Fox declared he was going to fish for perch for the ladies. And Brer Rabbit winked at Brer Turtle and said he was going to fish for suckers.

So everyone got busy with their hooks and their lines and their bait, and Brer Rabbit went to cast his line first. "I don't believe it!" he gasped, peering into the water and scratching his head. "The moon has done gone and fell in the water!"

Everyone looked serious and gathered round and tut-tutted and well-welled and my-myed as they looked into the pond and saw the moon floating there like a big pale coin. "There ain't no fish gonna come swimmin' through this water unless we get the moon out of the way," said Brer Rabbit. "Isn't that so, Brer Turtle?"

"Yep," nodded Brer Turtle, with a twinkle in his eye.

"So how we gonna get the moon out, Brer Rabbit?" worried Miss Meadows.

"Hmm," pondered Brer Rabbit, thoughtfully. "I've got it! We borrow Brer Turtle's drag net, and we drag it across the pond, and we drag the moon right out!"

"That's it!" breathed everyone, excitedly.

"That's surely it!"

"It don't bother you none if we borrow your drag net, does it Brer Turtle?"asked Brer Rabbit.

"Nope," replied Brer Turtle, trying hard not to collapse into laughter.

Then Brer Rabbit leapt off to fetch Brer Turtle's drag net and was back again before anyone could say 'lickety-spit'. "I think I'd better be the one to do the dragging," Brer Rabbit sighed. "It needs someone mighty clever and mighty muscley."

At that, Brer Fox and Brer Bear and Brer Wolf sprang forward and insisted on taking the drag net from Brer Rabbit. After all, they didn't want to look like saps in front of the ladies, now, did they?

Brer Fox and Brer Bear and Brer Wolf walked gingerly down to the edge of the pond with the net. They cast it into the water, dragged it along, and heaved it out, dripping. When the ripples had settled on the pond, there was the moon, shining just as bright in the water as before.

"Nope!" cried Brer Rabbit. "You need to go deeper."

Brer Fox and Brer Bear and Brer Wolf waded knee-deep into the cold pond. Once again they cast out the drag net, and once again they pulled it in without having caught the moon.

"Try again a little deeper," yelled Brer Rabbit from the nice, dry bank. "You'll surely get it next time." And Miss Meadows and Miss Motts eagerly waved them further out.

Brer Fox and Brer Bear and Brer Wolf took one more step and

suddenly the bottom of the pond fell away steeply and there was no more mud under their feet and they were ducked right under the water! Up they popped, choking and splashing and spluttering.

Miss Meadows and Miss Motts giggled and snickered as Brer Fox and Brer Bear and Brer Wolf hauled themselves out of the pond. They were a sight for sore eyes, dripping water from every hair and covered all-over in waterweed.

I've heard that the moon will always bite if you use fools for bait, Brer Rabbit giggled, looking them up and down. Now if you're asking me, "you gentlemen ought to get yourselves home and into some dry clothes,". And as Brer Fox and Brer Bear and Brer Wolf slopped and slapped away into the moonlight, Brer Turtle and Brer Rabbit went home with the girls.

THE LAST OF THE DRAGONS

by E Nesbit

Of course you know that dragons were once as common as motor-omnibuses are now, and almost as dangerous. But as every well brought-up prince was expected to kill a dragon, and rescue a princess, the dragons grew fewer and fewer till it was often quite hard for a princess to find a dragon to be rescued from. And at last there were no more dragons in France and no more dragons in Germany, or Spain, or Italy, or Russia. There were some left in China, and are still, but they are cold and bronzy, and there were never any, of course, in America. But the last real live dragon left was in England, and of course that was a very long time ago, before what you call English history began. This dragon lived in Cornwall in the big caves amidst the rocks, and a very fine dragon it was, quite seventy feet long from the tip of its fearful snout to the end of its terrible tail. It breathed fire and smoke, and rattled when it walked, because its scales were made of iron. Its wings were like half-umbrellas – or like bat's wings, only several thousand time bigger. Everyone was very frightened of it, and well they might be.

Now the King of Cornwall had one daughter, and when she

was sixteen, of course she would have to go and face the dragon: such tales are always told in royal nurseries at twilight, so the Princess knew what she had to expect. The dragon would not eat her, of course – because the prince would come and rescue her. But the Princess could not help thinking it would be much pleasanter to have nothing to do with the dragon at all – not even to be rescued from him. "All the princes I know are such very silly little boys," she told her father. "Why must I be rescued by a prince?"

"It's always done, my dear," said the King, taking his crown off and putting it on the grass, for they were alone in the garden, and even kings must unbend sometimes.

"Father, darling," said the Princess presently, when she had made a daisy chain and put it on the King's head, where the crown ought to have been. "Father, darling, couldn't we tie up one of the silly little princes for the dragon to look at – and then I could go and kill the dragon and rescue the prince? I fence much better than any of the princes we know."

"What an unladylike idea!" said the King, and put his crown on again, for he saw the Prime Minister coming with a basket of new-laid Bills for him to sign. "Dismiss the thought, my child. I rescued your mother from a dragon, and you don't want to set yourself up above her, I should hope?"

"But this is the last dragon. It is different from all other dragons."

"How?" asked the King.

"Because he is the last," said the Princess, and went off to her fencing lessons, with which she took great pains. She took great pains with all her lessons – for she could not give up the idea of fighting for the dragon. She took such pains that she became the strongest and boldest and most skilful and most sensible princess in Europe. She had always been the prettiest and nicest.

And the days and years went on, till at last the day came which was the day before the Princess was to be rescued from the dragon. The prince who was to do this deed of valour was a pale prince, with large eyes and a head full of mathematics and philosophy, but he had unfortunately neglected his fencing lessons. He was to stay the night at the palace, and there was a banquet.

After supper the Princess sent her pet parrot to the prince with a note. It said:

Please, Prince, come on to the terrace. I want to talk to you without anybody else hearing. – The Princess.

So, of course, he went – and he saw her gown of silver a long way off shining among the shadows of the trees like water in starlight. And when he came quite close to her he said: "Princess, at your service," and bent his cloth-of-gold-covered knee and put his hand on his cloth-of-gold-covered heart.

"Do you think," said the Princess earnestly, "that you will be able to kill the dragon?"

"I will kill the dragon," said the Prince firmly, "or perish in the attempt."

"It's no use your perishing," said the Princess.

"It's the least I can do," said the Prince.

"What I'm afraid of is that it'll be the most you can do," said the Princess.

"It's the only thing I can do," said he, "unless I kill the dragon."

"Why should you do anything for me is what I can't see," said she.

"But I want to," he said. "You must know that I love you better than anything in the world."

When he said that he looked so kind that the Princess began to like him a little.

"Look, here," she said, "no one else will go out tomorrow. You know they tie me to a rock and leave me – and then everybody scurries home and puts up the shutters and keeps them shut till you ride through the town in triumph shouting that you've killed the dragon, and I ride on the horse behind you weeping for joy."

"I've heard that this is how it is done," said he.

"Well, do you love me well enough to come very quickly and set me free – and we'll fight the dragon together?"

"It wouldn't be safe for you."

"Much safer for both of us for me to be free, with a sword in my hand, than tied up and helpless. Do agree."

He could refuse her nothing. So he agreed. And next day everything happened as she had said.

When he had cut the cords that tied her to the rock they stood on the lonely mountain-side looking at each other.

"It seems to me," said the Prince, "that this ceremony could have been arranged without the dragon."

"Yes," said the Princess, "but since it has been arranged with the dragon –"

"It seems such a pity to kill the dragon – the last in the world," said the Prince.

"Well then, don't let's," said the Princess, "let's tame it not to eat princesses but to eat out of their hands. They say everything can be tamed by kindness."

"Taming by kindness means giving them things to eat," said the Prince. "Have you got anything to eat?"

She hadn't, but the Prince owned that he had a few biscuits. "Breakfast was so very early," said he, "and I thought you might have felt faint after the fight."

"How clever," said the Princess, and they took a biscuit in each hand. And they looked here, and they looked there, but never a dragon could they see.

"But here's its trail," said the Prince, and pointed to where the rock was scarred and scratched so as to make a track leading to a dark cave. It was like cart-ruts in a Sussex road, mixed with the marks of sea-gulls' feet on the sea-sand. "Look, that's where it's dragged its brass tail and planted its steel claws."

"Don't let's think how hard its tail and its claws are," said the Princess, "or I shall begin to be frightened – and I know you can't tame anything, even by kindness, if you're frightened of it. Come on. Now or never."

She caught the Prince's hand in hers and they ran along the path towards the dark mouth of the cave. But they did not run into it. It really was so very dark.

So they stood aside, and the Prince shouted: "What ho! Dragon there! What ho within!" And from the cave they heard an answering voice and great clattering and creaking. It sounded as though a rather large cotton-mill was stretching itself and waking up out of its sleep.

The Prince and the Princess trembled, but they stood firm.

"Dragon – I say, dragon!" said the Princess, "do come out and talk to us. We've brought you a present."

"Oh yes – I know your presents," growled the dragon in a huge rumbling voice. "One of those precious princesses, I suppose? And I've got to come out and fight for her. Well, I tell you straight, I'm not going to do it. A fair fight I wouldn't say no to – a fair fight and no favour – but one of these put-up fights where you've got to lose – no! So I tell you. If I wanted a princess I'd come and take her, in my own time – but I don't. What do you suppose I'd do with her, if I'd got her?"

"Eat her, wouldn't you?" said the Princess, in a voice that trembled a little.

"Eat a fiddle-stick end," said the dragon very rudely. "I wouldn't touch the horrid thing."

The Princess's voice grew firmer.

"Do you like biscuits?" she said.

"No," growled the dragon.

"Not the nice little expensive ones with sugar on the top?"

"No," growled the dragon.

"Then what do you like?" asked the Prince.

"You go away and don't bother me," growled the dragon, and they could hear it turn over, and the clang and clatter of its turning echoed in the cave like the sound of the steam-hammers in the Arsenal at Woolwich.

The Prince and Princess looked at each other. What were they to do? Of course it was no use going home and telling the King that the dragon didn't want princesses – because His Majesty was very old-fashioned and would never have believed that a new-fashioned dragon could ever be at all different from an old-fashioned dragon. They could not go into the cave and kill the dragon. Indeed, unless he attacked the Princess it did not seem fair to kill him at all.

"He must like something," whispered the Princess, and she called out in a voice as sweet as honey and sugar-cane:

"Dragon! Dragon dear!"

"WHAT?" shouted the dragon. "Say that again!" and they could hear the dragon coming towards them through the darkness of the cave. The Princess shivered, and said in a very small voice:

"Dragon – Dragon dear!"

And then the dragon came out. The Prince drew his sword, and the Princess drew hers – the beautiful silver-handled one that the Prince had brought in his motor-car. But they did not attack; they moved back as the dragon came out, all the vast scaly length of him, and lay along the rock – his great wings halfspread and his silvery sheen gleaming like diamonds in the sun. At last they could retreat no further – the dark rock behind them stopped their way – and with their backs to the rock they stood swords in hand and waited.

The dragon drew nearer and nearer – and now they could see that he was breathing fire and smoke as they had expected – he came crawling slowly towards them wriggling a little as a puppy does when it wants to play and isn't quite sure whether you're not cross with it.

And then they saw that great tears were coursing down its brazen cheek.

"Whatever's the matter?" said the Prince.

"Nobody" sobbed the dragon, "ever called me 'dear' before!"

"Don't cry, dragon dear," said the Princess. "We'll call you 'dear' as often as you like. We want to tame you."

"I am tame," said the dragon – "that's just it. That's what nobody but you has ever found out. I'm so tame that I'd eat out of your hands."

"Eat what, dragon dear?" said the Princess. "Not biscuits?" The dragon slowly shook his heavy head.

"Your kindness quite undragons me," it said. "No one has ever asked any of us what we like to eat – always offering us princesses, and then rescuing them – and never once, 'What'll you take to drink the King's health in?' Cruel hard I call it," and it wept again.

"But what would you like to drink our health in?" said the Prince. "We're going to be married today, aren't we, Princess?"

She said that she supposed so.

"What'll I take to drink your health in?" asked the dragon. "Ah, you're something like a gentleman, you are sir. I don't mind if I do sir. I'll be proud to drink your and your good lady's health in a tiny drop of" – its voice faltered – "to think of you asking me so friendly like," it said. "Yes, sir, just a tiny drop of puppuppuppuppupetrol – tha-that's what does a dragon good, sir –"

"I've lots in the car," said the Prince and was off down the mountain like a flash. He was a good judge of character and knew that with this dragon the Princess would be safe. "If I might make so bold," said the dragon, "while the gentleman's away – p'raps just to pass the time you'd be so kind as to call me Dear again, and if you'd shake claws with a poor old dragon that's never been anybody's enemy but his own – well, the last of the dragons'll be the proudest dragon that's ever been since the first of them."

It held out an enormous paw, and the great steel hooks that were its claws closed over the Princess's hand as softly as the claws of the Himalayan bear will close over the bit of bun you hand it through the bars at the zoo.

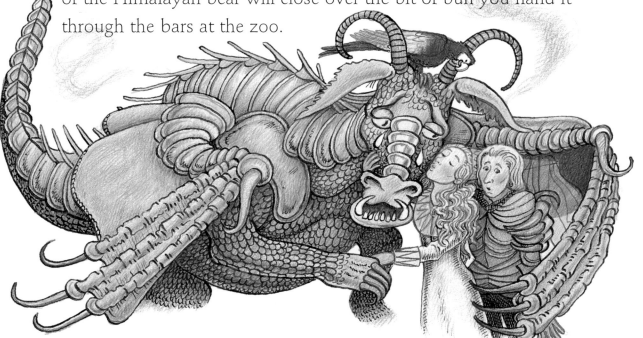

And so the Prince and Princess went back to the palace in triumph, the dragon following them like a pet dog. And all through the wedding festivities no one drank more earnestly to the happiness of the bride and bridegroom than the Princess's pet dragon – whom she had at once name Fido.

And when the happy pair were settled in their own kingdom, Fido came to them and begged to be allowed to make himself useful.

"There must be something I can do," he said, rattling his wings and stretching his claws. "My wings and claws and so on ought to be turned to some account – to say nothing of my grateful heart."

So the Prince had a special saddle or howdah made for him – very long it was – like the tops of many tramcars fitted together. One hundred and fifty seats were fitted to this, and the dragon, whose greatest pleasure was now to give pleasure to others, delighted in taking parties of children to the sea-side. It flew through the air quite easily with its hundred and fifty little passengers – and would lie on the sand patiently waiting till they were ready to return. The children were very fond of it, and used to call it Dear, a word which never failed to bring tears of affection and gratitude to its eyes. So it lived, useful and respected, till quite the other day – when someone happened to say, in his hearing, that dragons were out-of-date, now so much new machinery had come in. This so distressed him that he asked the King to change him into something less old-fashioned, and the kindly monarch at once changed him in to a mechanical contrivance. The dragon, indeed, became the first aeroplane.

Giants, Witches and Genies

THE GIANT WHO THREW TANTRUMS
by David L Harrison

At the foot of Thistle Mountain lay a village. In the village lived a little boy who liked to go walking. One Saturday afternoon he was walking in the woods when he was startled by a terrible noise. He scrambled quickly behind a bush.

Before long a huge giant came stamping down the path. He looked upset. "Tanglebangled ringlepox!" the giant bellowed. He banged his head against a tree until the leaves shook off like snowflakes. "Franglewhangled whippersnack!" the giant roared. Yanking up the tree, he whirled it around his head and knocked down twenty-seven other trees. Muttering to himself, he stalked up the path towards the top of Thistle Mountain.

The little boy hurried home. "I just saw a giant throwing a tantrum!" he told everyone in the village.

They only smiled.

"There's no such thing as a giant," the mayor assured him.

"He knocked down twenty-seven trees," said the little boy.

"Must have been a tornado," the weatherman said with a nod. "Happens around here all the time."

The next Saturday afternoon the little boy again went walking. Before long he heard a horrible noise. Quick as lightning, he slipped behind a tree.

Soon the same giant came storming down the path. He still looked upset.

"Pollywogging frizzelsnatch!" he yelled. Throwing himself down, he pounded the ground with both fists.

Boulders bounced like hailstones. Scowling, the giant puckered his lips into an "O". He drew in his breath sharply. It sounded like somebody slurping soup. "Pooh!" he cried. Grabbing his left foot with both hands, the giant hopped on his right foot up the path towards the top of Thistle Mountain.

The little boy hurried home. "That giant's at it again," he told everyone. "He threw such a tantrum that the ground trembled!"

"Must have been an earthquake," the police chief said. "Happens around here sometimes."

The next Saturday afternoon the little boy again went walking.Before long he heard a frightening noise. He dropped down behind a rock.

Soon the giant came fuming down the path. When he reached the little boy's rock, he puckered his lips into an "O". He drew in his breath sharply with a loud, rushing-wind sound. "Phooey!" he cried. "I never get it right!" The giant held his breath until his face turned blue and his eyes rolled up. "Fozzlehumper backawacket! he panted. Then he lumbered up the path towards the top of Thistle Mountain.

The little boy followed him. Up and up and up he climbed to the very top of Thistle Mountain. There he discovered a huge cave. A surprising sound was coming from it. The giant was crying!

"All I want is to whistle," he sighed through his tears. "But every time I try, it comes out wrong!"

The little boy had just learned to whistle. He knew how hard it could be. He stepped inside the cave.

The giant looked surprised. "How did you get here?"

"I know what you're doing wrong," the little boy said.

When the giant heard that, he leaned down and put his hands on his knees. "Tell me at once!" he begged.

"You have to stop throwing tantrums," the little boy told him.

"I promise!" said the giant, who didn't want anyone to think he had poor manners.

"Pucker your lips …" the little boy said.

"I always do!" the giant assured him.

"Then blow," the little boy added.

"Blow?"

"Blow."

The giant looked as if he didn't believe  it. He puckered his lips into an "O". He blew. Out came a long, low whistle. It sounded like a railway engine. The giant smiled. He shouted, "I whistled! Did you hear that? I whistled!" Taking the little boy's hand, he danced in a circle. "You're a good friend," the giant said.

"Thank you," said the little boy. "Perhaps some time we can whistle together. But just now I have to go. It's my suppertime."

The giant stood before his cave and waved good-bye.

The little boy seldom saw the giant after that. But the giant kept his promise about not throwing tantrums.

"We never have earthquakes," the mayor liked to say.

"Haven't had a tornado in ages," the weatherman would add.

Now and then they heard a long, low whistle somewhere in the distance.

"Must be a train," the police chief would say.

But the little boy knew his friend the giant was walking up the path towards the top of Thistle Mountain – whistling.

BABA YAGA, THE BONY-LEGGED
a Russian folk tale

There was once a wicked woman who hated her stepdaughter so much that she pushed the little girl out of doors and told her to go and borrow a needle and thread from Baba Yaga, the bony-legged witch. The girl's stepmother did it when her husband was out at work, so the little girl had no one to turn to and she was terrified. Baba Yaga had iron teeth, and lived in the middle of the deep, dark forest, in a hut which moved about on hens' legs. Neverthless, the girl dared not disobey her cruel stepmother. So off she went into the deep, dark forest.

The little girl was soon among tall, prickly trees that whispered all around her, and she quite forgot which way was which. Big tears began to glisten in her eyes.

"Do not weep, little girl," came a cheerful voice. The little girl looked up to see that a little nightingale was talking to her. "You are a kind-hearted girl and I will tell you what I can to help you. Pick up any things that you come across along the path and make sure you use them wisely."

So the little girl set off again, further into the deep, dark forest.

As she walked along, she saw a neatly folded handkerchief lying among the pine-needles, and she put it in her pocket. A little further on, she took some ribbons that were dangling from the branches. A few steps on, she picked up a little can of oil that lay amongst some rocks. Next, she came across a big, juicy bone and then a large maple-leaf sprinkled with some tasty-looking morsels of meat – and then her pocket was full.

It wasn't long before some big iron gates came into view up ahead, and beyond them was Baba Yaga's hut, running about on its hens' legs. The little girl shivered with fear. Suddenly a howling wind rose up which sent the branches of the trees whipping fiercely around her head. *I'll never get near that horrible hut at this rate*, the little girl realised, ducking the boughs coming at her thick and fast. She thought quickly. She pulled out the ribbons and tied them onto the trees, and as soon as she did so, the wind dropped to a gentle breeze and the branches became still.

Then the little girl tried to push open the gates, but a dreadful creaking and groaning tore the air. The girl took the oil can from her pocket and gave the hinges a good oiling. After that, the gate opened without a squeak, and the girl passed through.

All of a sudden, a drooling, snarling dog came running at her out of nowhere, barking fit to wake the dead. Quick as a flash, the girl grabbed the big, juicy bone and threw it to the dog. He forgot his attack immediately and lay down and began to gnaw.

Now the girl faced the hut itself, scuttling about on its awful scaly legs. And there on the steps stood BABA YAGA THE BONY-LEGGED! "Come in, my dear!" grinned the witch, showing her iron teeth. "While I'm searching for that needle and thread you want, you can have a nice bath and do my spinning for me."

Baba Yaga gripped the girl's arm with her claw-like fingers and pulled her up the steps into the house. "Run her a bath and be quick about it!" she screamed at her pale-faced maid, before whispering "Make sure you scrub her well, all ready for eating." Then Baba Yaga the bony-legged bustled away.

The pale-faced maid began to hurry about filling the bath with water, and the little girl saw that she was trembling with fear of Baba Yaga the bony-legged. "I am sorry for you having to live and work here," the little girl said. "Here, have this handkerchief as a little present to cheer you up."

"Oh thank you," the pale-faced maid sighed, gazing in delight at the lovely embroidery. "I will use a teacup instead of a jug to fill the bath, so you have more time to escape."

Then the little girl noticed a skinny black cat in the corner. "You don't look as if you've eaten properly for ages," she said, stroking his tatty fur. "Here, have these scraps of meat."

"Oh thank you," the skinny black cat purred, neatly washing his paws. "I will do the spinning for you, so you have more time to escape. Now take this magic towel and comb and run for your life. When you hear Baba Yaga coming, throw each of them behind you, one by one."

So the little girl took the magic towel and comb and began to run for her life through the deep, dark forest, while the cat sat down at the spinning wheel, tangled the wool into a big mess and hid behind it, and began to spin.

Several times, the witch passed the open door of the room and peered in. But when she heard the whirr of the spinning wheel and saw the pile of tangled wool, she went away content that the little girl was working hard. But by and by, the witch began to get suspicious that the pile of wool wasn't getting any smaller. "Are you sure you know how to spin properly, little girl?" she screeched.

"Yes, thank you," yowled the cat, trying to sound like the little girl but failing terribly. Then Baba Yaga the bony-legged screamed with fury. She rushed into the room and grabbed the cat by the scruff of the neck. "Why did you let the girl escape?" she howled.

"You've never given me anything to eat but left-overs," the cat hissed. "That kind-hearted girl gave me tasty morsels of meat."

Then Baba Yaga stalked over to the pale-faced maid and slapped her. "Why did you let the girl escape?" she howled.

"You've never given me a single present," the pale-faced maid shouted. "That kind-hearted girl gave me a lovely hanky."

Then Baba Yaga stormed outside and threw a stick at the dog. "Why did you let the girl escape?" she howled.

"You've never given me a bone," the dog barked. "That kind-hearted girl gave me a big, juicy one to chew on."

Then Baba Yaga kicked the iron gates. "Why did you let the girl escape?" she howled.

"You've let us get all stiff and rusty," they creaked. "That kind-hearted girl soothed our aching joints with lots of lovely oil."

Finally, Baba Yaga punched the birch trees. "Why did you let the girl escape?" she howled.

"You've never once decorated our branches," they roared, "but that kind-hearted girl tied beautiful ribbons all over us."

Then Baba Yaga gnashed her iron teeth and jumped on her broomstick and raced off through the deep, dark forest after the little girl. The little girl heard the swish of the air and knew she was coming and threw down the magic towel. Suddenly a wide rushing river appeared before Baba Yaga, splashing all over her broomstick and soaking it so badly that it could no longer fly. Spitting and cursing, Baba Yaga had to get off and slowly wade across. Then Baba Yaga was off and running . . .

The little girl heard the pounding of Baba Yaga's footsteps and knew she was coming, and she threw down the magic comb. All at once, a jungle sprang up in front of Baba Yaga, so thick and dense and tangled that Baba Yaga the bony-legged could do nothing to find her way through it. She squawked and screamed and gnashed her iron teeth, and stormed back to her horrible hut, shouting all the way.

The little girl saw her father standing at the door of their house, and she rushed to tell him all about her stepmother's evil plot. Her father pushed the wicked woman out of doors and drove her into the magic jungle – after which, she was never seen again. Then the little girl and her father lived happily on their own, and the nightingale came to visit every day.

THE SELFISH GIANT

retold from the original tale by Oscar Wilde

nce there was a beautiful garden in which the children used to play every day on their way home from school. The children didn't think that the beautiful garden belonged to anyone in particular. But one day a huge giant strode in and boomed, "What are you all doing here? This is MY garden. Get lost!" Seven years ago, the giant had gone to visit his friend the Cornish ogre. Now he was back and he wanted his garden all to himself.

Of course, the children ran away at once. But the giant wasn't satisfied. Straight away, he put up a high fence all the way around his garden with a noticeboard outside which read: TRESPASSERS WILL BE PROSECUTED. He really was a very selfish giant.

Now the poor children had nowhere to play. But the giant didn't give any thought to that. He was too busy wondering why the blossom had fallen from the trees, why the flowers had withered, and why all the birds seemed to have flown away. *Surely it is meant to be the springtime,* the giant thought to himself as he looked out of the window and saw huge flakes of snow beginning to tumble from the

sky. Frost painted the trees silver. A blanket of ice chilled the ground and hardened the plants into stiff, lifeless spikes. Day after day, the north wind roared around the giant's garden, zooming around his roof and howling down his chimney pots. And the hail came to visit too, battering on the giant's windows until the giant bellowed with annoyance and clapped his hands over his ears against the noisy rattling.

Then one Saturday, the giant woke up to hear a sound he had almost forgotten – it was a bird, chirruping and cheeping in his garden. A beautiful perfume tickled the giant's nose . . . It was the scent of flowers! "Spring has come at last!" the giant beamed, and he pulled on his clothes and ran outside into his garden.

The giant couldn't believe what he saw. The snow had melted, the frost and ice were gone, the sky was blue and the breeze was gentle and warm. And there were children everywhere. They had crept back into his garden through a hole that had worn away in the fence. Now children were sitting in trees heavy with ripe fruit. Playing among flowerbeds filled with nodding blossoms.

Running over emerald green grass scattered with daisies and buttercups. And the sound of their happy laughter filled the air.

Only in one corner of the garden was it still winter. A little boy was standing in a patch of snow, looking up at the bare branches of a chestnut tree and crying because he couldn't reach it. The giant's heart ached as he watched. "Now I know what makes my garden beautiful," the giant murmured. "It is the children. How selfish I have been!"

The giant strode through the garden towards the sobbing little boy. The giant scooped him up gently and set him among the icy boughs of the chestnut tree. At once, broad green leaves appeared all over the branches and down below, the snow vanished and it was spring. The little boy's face brightened into a huge smile and he reached his arms up around the giant's neck and hugged him.

"It is your garden now, little children," laughed the giant, and the children skipped about delightedly. The giant took his axe and knocked down the fence and had more fun than he had ever had in his life by playing with them all day. Only one thing spoiled the giant's new happiness. He looked all over his garden for the little boy whom he had helped into the tree, but he was nowhere to be found. The giant loved the little boy the best, because he had kissed him, and he longed more than anything to see his friend again.

Many years passed by and the children came every day to play in the beautiful garden. The giant became old and creaky and eventually he could no longer run about and let the children climb over him as he had done. The giant sat in a special armchair so he could watch the children enjoying themselves. "My garden is very beautiful," he would say to himself, 'but the children are the most beautiful things of all." Sometimes the giant's huge grey head would nod forwards and he would begin to snore, and the children would creep away quietly so they didn't disturb him. And one afternoon, the giant woke from such a little doze to see an astonishing sight.

In the farthest corner of his garden was a golden tree he had never seen before. The giant's heart leaped for joy, for standing underneath it was the little boy he had loved.

The giant heaved himself up from his armchair and shuffled across the grass as fast as his old legs would take him. But when he drew near the little boy, his face grew black as thunder. There were wounds on the little boy's palms and on his feet. "Who has dared to hurt you?" boomed the giant. "Tell me, and I will go after them with my big axe!"

"These are the marks of love," the little boy smiled, and he took the giant's hand. "Once, you let me play in your garden," the little boy said. "And today, you shall come with me to mine, which is in Paradise."

And when the children came running to play that afternoon, they found the giant lying dead under the beautiful tree, covered with a blanket of snowy-white blossoms.

ALADDIN AND THE LAMP

a tale from The Arabian Nights

Aladdin's father had died years ago, abandoning Aladdin with no education, no job and no money. And so Aladdin lived life as a street urchin until there was a knock at his mother's door one evening and in strode a tall, turbaned man with a flowing cloak and the longest moustache Aladdin had ever seen.

"May Allah be praised! At last I have found you both!" the man cried, smiling broadly at Aladdin's mother. "I am Aladdin's long-lost uncle, a wealthy merchant, and I offer my nephew Aladdin the chance to come and work for me and make his fortune."

At this, Aladdin's mother's eyes opened wide and round. "I'm sure your father never mentioned a brother," she hissed under her breath to her son. "But don't be so foolish as to point it out!" And she set about making the merchant truly welcome.

Next morning, Aladdin was horrified to find that he was woken up at sunrise, forced to wash and tidy his hair, and pushed out of doors to begin his new career. Still half-asleep, he ran to keep up with his so-called uncle as he strode at a cracking pace through the bazaar, past the harbour, and right into the burning hot desert. "Find some

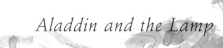

wood and build a fire," his uncle ordered, and from the tone of his voice, Aladdin thought it was best not to argue. His uncle scattered some strange-smelling powders into the flames and chanted words in a weird language. There was a blaze of green fire and the ground trembled under their feet. When the smoke cleared, a trapdoor had appeared in the earth before them.

Aladdin's uncle heaved it open and bellowed at Aladdin, "Go down and find me a lamp!"

Aladdin was frozen with fear. His teeth chattered and his knees knocked with terror at all that had happened.

"You useless boy!" Aladdin's uncle roared, sounding highly like Aladdin's mother. He took a ring from his hand and shoved it roughly onto Aladdin's finger. "This magic ring will keep you safe. Now go!" And he pushed Aladdin through the trapdoor and onto the staircase.

Down, down, down into the darkness went Aladdin. He hurried through several gloomy caves and finally reached a beautiful garden. Many trees were growing there, covered in brightly coloured fruits. Aladdin couldn't resist picking handfuls of the glassy fruits and filling his pockets and shirt. He gasped with relief as he saw a rusty lamp resting on the grass, and he stuffed that into his shirt too. Then he was off back through the caves . . .

Now Aladdin hadn't spent all that time on the streets without becoming very streetwise. He was highly suspicious about his so-called uncle and, of course, Aladdin's suspicions were right. The merchant was in fact an evil sorcerer who knew powerful black magic. The sorcerer's wicked arts had shown him the whereabouts of the cave and the powers of the secret lamp that lay within, and he had worked hard for years to try to find a way in. Eventually, the sorcerer discovered that no one was allowed to enter the cave and take the lamp for themselves. Someone else had to do it for them – someone like a street-urchin, who wouldn't be missed. Because that someone had to remain locked in the cave forever!

Now Aladdin could see the sorcerer's eyes glinting greedily down through the square hole that led to the upper world. "Give me the lamp!" the sorcerer barked.

All Aladdin wanted to do was to get out of there as quickly as possible. "Help me out first and then I'll give it to you," he shouted back.

"I said, give me the lamp!" the sorcerer insisted.

Aladdin wasn't stupid. "Sure," he yelled, "just as soon as you get me out of here!"

"GIVE ME THE LAMP, YOU STUPID BOY!" roared the sorcerer.

Well, that did it. Aladdin hated people telling him he was worthless. "NO!" he shouted. "I found it and now I'm going to keep it!"

The sorcerer hopped about with rage, cursing and spluttering. "Then have it," he screamed, "and enjoy it in the darkness forever!" He thundered out the magic words and the trapdoor slammed shut with a massive crash. When Aladdin put his hands up and felt about, the opening was gone.

"What have I done!" Aladdin moaned, wringing his hands. As he did so, he happened to rub the sorcerer's ring. There was a blinding flash and a huge genie stood before him.

"I am the genie of the ring!" the massive apparition thundered. "Speak your wish, O master, and I will obey."

"I wish to heaven I was out of this cave!" Aladdin howled.

At once, Aladdin found himself back on the sands of the desert, blinking in the hot sunlight. He raced home and blurted out his whole sorry adventure to his mother. At first she thought he was telling one of his usual stories, but then Aladdin showed her the multi-coloured glass fruits and rusty old lamp.

"If we sell these glittery baubles and this old lamp," his mother sighed, "we'll at least have some pennies to buy some bread and cheese to go with our soup tonight."

"But we won't get the best price for the lamp unless I try to clean it up a bit," said Aladdin. He picked it up and began to rub at it with his sleeve.

Once more, there was a blinding flash and a genie even bigger than the genie of the ring stood before him. "I am the genie of the lamp!" roared the enormous spirit. "Speak your wish, O master, and I will obey."

"Bring us some food!" was the starving Aladdin's command.

Suddenly there was a table before them, covered with huge golden platters laden with delicious food. Aladdin and his mother could hardly believe their eyes. In a few minutes, their stomachs were more full than they had been in years. And after they'd sold one of the gold platters in the market, their purses were too.

After that, the lives of Aladdin and his mother changed for the better. They were clever not to arouse suspicion by selling the gold platters only one at a time, when their purses were becoming empty. No one would have called them rich, although they lived much more comfortably than they had before. And so life would probably have gone on, if Aladdin hadn't been caught up in town one day in a great procession. Hundreds of slaves with swords at their sides came marching through the bazaar, and in the middle of them, high on their shoulders, was a magnificent litter of gold and silver. As the litter was carried past Aladdin, the swishing silk curtains swung just a little to one side, and inside Aladdin glimpsed the beautiful Princess Balroubadour.

From that moment on, Aladdin was head over heels in love. He couldn't speak, he couldn't eat, he couldn't sleep, for thinking of the beautiful Princess Balroubadour. Aladdin's mother watched her son grow thinner and paler by the day, and finally decided she had to do something about it – even if it was the most foolish thing she had ever done in her life. She loaded up one of the golden platters with the coloured, glassy fruits that Aladdin had brought back from the sorcerer's cave, and she went to see the princess's father – the Sultan of Baghdad himself!

Of course, the sultan realised what the jewels were at once – and he had never seen such huge, fine diamonds, emeralds, rubies and sapphires in his life. Being a greedy man, and hoping that there were more where those came from, he agreed at once that Aladdin should marry his daughter and become his son-in-law.

Aladdin was overjoyed, and that night he dared to use the lamp once more and conjure up the genie. By morning, a splendid palace with golden domes and pearl spires and nine hundred and ninety-

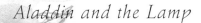

nine stained glass windows had been built exactly opposite the sultan's own palace. The sultan clapped his hands with delight, the wedding festivities were held that very afternoon, and Aladdin took his beautiful bride to live in his splendid new home.

It was fortunate that Princess Balroubadour felt the same way about Aladdin as he felt about her, and together they were completely happy – until one day, when Aladdin was out hunting, a ragged old pedlar came through the streets of the bazaar shouting, "New lamps for old! New lamps for old!" The princess and her maid rushed to the eighty-eighth window of the palace to look out on the funny little man who was offering to swap good wares for bad.

"How silly!" the maid giggled, and rushed to exchange the rusty old lamp in Aladdin's room. As soon as Aladdin's lamp was in the pedlar's hands, he gave a little cry of excitement and disappeared through the streets. A few seconds later, the princess, her maid and the entire palace had vanished, too! As you have probably guessed, the pedlar was none other than the wicked sorcerer.

Aladdin returned from his hunting trip to find his wife missing, his palace gone and his father-in-law furious! "Bring me my daughter within forty days," the Sultan roared, "or I'll stuff your precious jewels into your mouth and make you eat them!"

Worst of all, Aladdin no longer had his wonderful lamp. "What am I going to do?" he moaned, standing all alone in the spot where his palace had once been. He wrung his hands in despair, and as he did so, he rubbed the sorcerer's magic ring. In a flash, the genie of the ring stood before him once more. "Speak your wish, O master, and I will obey," boomed the mighty spirit.

"Bring back my palace, with everyone and everything in it!" yelped the delighted Aladdin.

But the genie shook his head firmly and said, "I cannot, master. The palace is under the power of the genie of the lamp."

Aladdin thought hard for a couple of seconds and then his face brightened. "Then take me to my wife!" he yelled.

Suddenly, Aladdin was standing in his palace in front of his startled – but overjoyed – wife. "Hurry," Princess Balroubadour urged. "The sorcerer is out at the moment, but he keeps the lamp with him at all times. We have to think of a way to get it from him."

The quickwitted Aladdin mixed a sleeping powder into a goblet of wine, gave it to the princess, and then hid behind a screen. Only a few moments later, the sorcerer came striding in, his cloak billowing out behind him. The smiling Princess Balroubadour rushed to offer him a refreshing drink – and as soon as the sorcerer had thirstily drained the sleeping potion, he collapsed on the floor in a crumpled heap.

Aladdin sprang out from behind the screen and fumbled in the sorcerer's clothes. At last, he held his wonderful lamp in his hands! He rubbed it . . . gave the order . . . and in the twinkling of an eye, he, his wife, his palace – and the sorcerer – were back in Baghdad.

Aladdin and Princess Balroubadour breathed a sigh of relief. "I don't know about you," Aladdin said to his beautiful bride, "but I've had quite enough magic for one lifetime – and besides, now I've got you, I've got everything in the world I could possibly want."

The princess nodded her agreement, and Aladdin once more rubbed his wonderful lamp. "I give you your freedom!" he told the genie, and in a blinding flash the overjoyed spirit was gone from the lamp forever.

Aladdin and the Princess Balroubadour (and of course, Aladdin's mum) lived happily ever after. And when the sorcerer eventually woke up, he got what he had always wanted – the rusty old lamp, no more and no less.

IN THE CASTLE OF GIANT CRUELTY

retold from an original tale in John Bunyan's
The Pilgrim's Progress

There was once a dark, ugly city where no one seemed to be happy. But none of the grumpy, scowling citizens ever thought of leaving because they knew nothing of life outside the city walls. Huge, flat plains of mud surrounded the city as far as the eye could see. No one had ever braved the danger of trying to wade through them, so no one even knew if there was anything beyond the swamps. There were rumours of a far distant city where the sun always shone and where the people lived happily together – but no one really believed it existed . . . that is, except for a man called Christian.

For a long time, Christian had been growing more and more miserable with his life in the grim, depressing city. But it was the strange, glowing light that finally made him decide to leave. It was some weeks ago that Christian had first glimpsed the light, far away in the distance, beyond the mud flats. No one else seemed to be able to see it. They just shuffled around with their hands in their pockets, looking at the pavements as usual. But Christian thought the light was beautiful. "I shall leave this dreadful city and somehow reach the place the light is coming from," he decided. "Or I shall die in the attempt," he added.

Christian didn't take anything with him. He just got up the next morning and instead of making his usual way to work, he walked towards the gates that led out of the city. As people realised that Christian meant to leave town, they began to laugh and jeer at him. "You must be mad!" they mocked. "You'll be floundering in that mud by nightfall and no one will come to rescue you!" But Christian didn't listen to them. He just heaved open the rusty, creaky city gates and strode out into the swamps.

As soon as Christian was outside the city, he felt as if he had left his cares and troubles behind him. Determinedly, he began walking towards the light in the distance. He walked . . . and walked . . . and walked . . . until he had left the city so far behind that he

couldn't see its dark, smoky outline any more. He walked and walked until he dropped with thirst and hunger and exhaustion. Christian didn't have the strength to lift himself back up. He closed his eyes and everything went black.

It was having a huge bucket of water sloshed over his face that finally brought Christian back to his senses. He sat bolt upright, gasping and choking and spluttering out the iciness that filled his nose and mouth.

"I am the Giant Cruelty!" boomed the loudest voice that Christian had ever heard. He looked up and began to tremble. He was in a stone room the size of a cave, and standing over him was a man as tall as his house back in the city. The giant had blood-shot eyes and blackened teeth and long, claw-like nails. "What were you doing, trespassing on my land?" Giant Cruelty thundered.

"I'm v-v-very s-s-s-orry," Christian stuttered. "I d-d-didn't realise I was trespassing."

"That is a pitiful excuse!" the giant bellowed. "Now you are no longer a trespasser. You are a prisoner.." The giant's eyes lit up with amusement and he cackled evilly. "I shall enjoy watching you rot in my dungeons!" he boomed, and scooped Christian up in his mighty fist.

Christian's heart thumped as he felt himself being carried down a long flight of steps. He shivered at the echoing of the giant's footsteps all around and at the damp chill in the air. He wrinkled his nose in disgust as a vile stench filled his nostrils.

Suddenly, the giant's fist opened and Christian was thrown onto the stone floor of a dungeon. A rat scampered up and squeaked in his face, and Christian sprang to his feet with shock.

"Have this bread and water," Giant Cruelty ordered, hurling a mouldy loaf at Christian and slamming down a bucket of foul-smelling water. "You have to stay alive so I can come back tomorrow and watch you scream and cry and beg for mercy."

Giant Cruelty chuckled. He slammed the door of the dungeon, locked it with a massive iron key, and stomped back up the stairs.

Christian swallowed hard and turned away from the locked door. He wasn't the only prisoner after all. Six faces peered out at him from the shadows – faces that looked even more hungry and thirsty and despairing than his own.

"How long have you been here?" Christian gulped.

"So long that we have forgotten our own names," one man sighed.

"The giant only feeds us once a week," a woman whimpered, eyeing Christian's bread and water.

"Here," Christian decided at once. "Come and join in my share with me. If we all stay strong and help each other, maybe we can find a way out of here together."

The desperate men and women didn't need inviting twice. They crept out of the shadows and fell on the loaf ravenously.

At that very moment, a spine-tingling CREAK! filled the air and the dungeon door swung wide open. To Christian's astonishment, a golden key had appeared in the lock. There were words down the shaft which read: the Key of Kindness.

Christian didn't stop to wonder at the strange key. He just grabbed it and urged, "Come on everybody!", and hurried everyone out of the dungeon and up the stairs. The Key of Kindness somehow fitted every locked door they came to and the giant seemed to have disappeared altogether.

Christian and his new friends didn't stop running until they had left the castle far behind them. Then they hugged each other, panting, and turned towards the glowing light. Christian smiled. Now he could see the faint outline of a golden city – and it was much, much closer than before. As he set off on his journey once more, he felt a new feeling in his heart. It was hope.

A NEW ARRIVAL

from Ms Wiz Spells Trouble by Terence Blacker

Most teachers are strange and the teachers at St Barnabas School were no exception.

Yet it's almost certain that none of them – not Mr Gilbert, the headmaster, who liked to pick his nose during Assembly, not Mrs Hicks who talked to her teddies in class, not Miss Gomaz who smoked cigarettes in the lavatory – none of them was quite as odd as the new form teacher for Class Three.

Some of the children in Class Three thought she was a witch. Others said she was a hippy. A few of them thought she was just a bit mad. But they all agreed that there had never been anyone quite like her at St Barnabas before.

This is her story. I wonder what you think she was . . .

As soon as their new teacher walked into the classroom on the first day of term, the children of Class Three sensed that there was something different about her. She was quite tall, with long black hair and bright green eyes. She wore tight jeans with a purple blouse. Her fingers were decorated with several large rings and black nail varnish.

She looked as if she was on her way to a disco, not teaching at a school.

Most surprising of all, she wasn't frightened. Class Three were known in the school as the "problem class". It had a reputation for being difficult and noisy, for having what was called a "disruptive element". Miss Jones, their last teacher, had left the school in tears. But none of that seemed to worry this strange looking new teacher.

"My name is Miss Wisdom," she said in a quiet but firm voice. "So what do you say to me every morning when I walk in?'

"Good morning, Miss Wisdom," said Class Three unenthusiastically.

"Wrong," said the teacher with a flash of her green eyes. "You say, 'Hi, Ms Wiz!'."

Jack, who was one of Class Three's Disruptive Element, giggled at the back of the class.

"Yo," he said in a silly American accent. "Why, hi Ms Wiz!"

Caroline, the class dreamer, was paying attention for a change.

"Why is it Ms . . . er, Ms?" she asked.

"Well," said Ms Wiz, "I'm not Mrs because I'm not married, thank goodness, and I'm not Miss because I think Miss sounds silly for a grown woman, don't you?"

"Not as silly as Ms," muttered Katrina, who liked to find fault wherever possible.

"And why Wiz?" asked a rather large boy sitting in the front row. It was Podge, who was probably the most annoying and certainly the greediest boy in the class.

"Wiz?" said Ms Wiz with a mysterious smile. "Just you wait and see."

Ms Wiz reached inside a big leather bag that she had placed beside her desk. She pulled out a china cat.

"That," she said, placing the cat carefully on her desk, "is my friend Hecate the Cat. She's watching you all the time. She sees everything and hears everything. She's my spy."

Ms Wiz turned to the blackboard.

"Weird," muttered Jack.

An odd, hissing sound came from the china cat. Its eyes lit up like torches.

"Hecate sees you even when my back is turned," said Ms Wiz, who now faced the class. "Will the person who said 'weird' spell it please?"

Everyone stared at Jack, who blushed.

"I.T.," he stammered.

No one laughed.

"Er, W . . . I . . ."

"Wrong," said Ms Wiz. "W.E.I.R.D. If you don't know how to spell a word, Jack, don't use it." She patted the china cat.

"Good girl, Hecate," she said.

"How did she know my name?" whispered Jack.

The new teacher smiled. "Children, remember one thing. Ms Wiz knows everything."

"Now," she said briskly. "Pay attention please. Talking of spelling, I'm going to give you a first lesson in casting spells."

"Oh, great," said Katrina grumpily. "Now we've got a witch for a teacher."

Hecate the cat hissed angrily.

"No, Katrina, not a witch," said Ms Wiz sharply. "We don't call them witches these days. It gives people the wrong idea. We call them Paranormal Operatives. Now – any suggestions for our first spell?"

Podge put up his hand immediately.

"Could we turn our crayons into lollipops, please Ms?" he asked.

"No," said Ms Wiz. "Spells are not for personal greed."

"How about turning Class Two into frogs?" asked Katrina.

"Nor are they for revenge. There will be no unpleasant spells around here while I'm your teacher," said Ms Wiz before adding, almost as an afterthought, "unless they're deserved, of course."

She looked up out of the window. In the playground Mr Brown, the School Caretaker, was sweeping up leaves.

"Please draw the playground," said Ms Wiz. "Imagine it without any leaves. The best picture will create the spell."

Almost for the first time in living memory, Class Three worked in complete quiet. Katrina didn't complain that someone had nicked her pencil. Caroline managed to concentrate on her work. Podge forgot to look in his trouser pocket for one last sweet. Not a single paper pellet was shot across the room by Jack.

At the end of the lesson, Ms Wiz looked at the drawings carefully.

"Well, they're all quite good," she

said eventually. "But I think I like Caroline's the best."

She took Caroline's drawing and carefully taped it to the window.

"Please close your eyes while I cast the spell," she said.

There was a curious humming noise as Class Three sat, eyes closed, in silence.

"Open," said Ms Wiz, after a few seconds. "Regard Caroline's work."

The children looked at Caroline's drawing. It looked exactly as it had before, except it was steaming slightly.

"Hey – look at the playground," shouted Katrina.

Everyone looked out of the window. To their amazement, the leaves on the ground had disappeared. Mr Brown stood by his wheelbarrow, scratching his head.

"Weird," said Jack. "Very weird indeed."

DAVID AND THE GIANT

a tale from the Old Testament of the Bible

How David wished he could be just like his three older brothers! They were away fighting in the war with the fierce Philistines. But David was too young to join the great army of King Saul, like them. He was too young to strap on his armour and gird on his sword and face the pagan warriors, like they had. He was too young to fight to defend his country and his religion, to fight for his God, like they were.

Well, that's what David's father, the white-haired Jesse, kept telling him, anyway. So David found himself stuck at home looking after his father's sheep and listening to his father worry day and night about his other sons away at the battlefront.

One evening, David returned home from his peaceful day out on the pastures to find that his father was packing some grain, bread and cheeses. "I'm sending you to take these supplies to your brothers, David," said old Jesse, with an anxious look on his face. "It will be a dangerous trip, and I'm in half a mind not to send you at all. But they can't have very much to keep them going – and besides, I'm desperate to hear news of how they are."

David's heart leapt within his chest. At last, he was going on an adventure! He tried not to look too excited to be leaving his old father all alone at home, but he couldn't help the bright glint in his eye as he waved goodbye and set off on his horse.

After several days of hard riding, David had gained a bruised bottom and an aching back, and had lost a little of his reckless enthusiasm. In fact, when David finally reached King Saul's army camp, he no longer felt very excited at all. He found the soldiers exhausted and running away from the battlefield as fast as their wobbly legs would carry them. The retreating troops threatened to trample David underfoot as they swarmed back into the camp, and David was very glad when he finally recognised the familiar faces of his brothers among the retreating troops. "Whatever is going on?" David gasped.

"It's a giant – a real, live giant!" one of his brothers panted. "Whenever we go out to face the Philistine army in a battle, their troops don't come out to meet us. Instead, they send the giant Goliath, who challenges us to settle things by a duel – just him against one of us. It sounds fair enough – but you ought to see the size of him! There's no way any one in their right mind would face him alone! So we run away and Goliath and the Philistines stand there hurling insults at us."

At that, little David felt his blood begin to boil. You mean to say that no one has tried to beat this giant? he marvelled. Our whole army is a laughing stock? And he marched off to find King Saul. At first, King Saul was highly amused when his guards showed a little shepherd boy into his tent, who demanded, "I want you to let me fight Goliath! God has given me the strength to fight lions and bears

when I'm looking after my sheep, and now he'll give me the strength to fight the giant, too!" There was a strange light of faith gleaming in the boy's eyes, so, much against his better judgement, King Saul decided to let the little shepherd boy have a go after all.

The king brought his own, very best, armour for David and helped dress him up in it. But the armour totally swamped him and he could hardly move in it. So David took the whole caboodle off again. There he stood in his simple shepherd's robe with his crook, his catapult and a bag of five round stones. And that's how he strode out to face the giant . . .

Goliath was far and away the biggest man that David had ever seen. He had legs like tree trunks and carried a spear the size of a battering ram. When the giant saw the tiny figure of the little shepherd boy coming out to meet him, he threw back his head and roared with laughter. Then he stomped forwards over the earth, ready to rip David apart like a rag doll.

David gulped as the mighty man came storming towards him. He could feel the ground shaking as the giant thundered nearer, and he set a stone onto his catapult. Now he could see the big scar on the giant's chin and the way his bristly eyebrows joined in the middle. David took aim and fired – WHAM! the little stone sank right into the centre of the giant's forehead.

"What happened?" Goliath gasped, as he collapsed.

He never found out, because David rushed up, drew the giant's own sword and hacked off the wicked giant's head. And King Saul's army chased the stunned Philistine soldiers all the way back to their own cities.

THE FISHERMAN AND THE BOTTLE

a tale from The Arabian Nights

The fisherman was having a very bad day. The first time he had cast his nets in to the Arabian Sea, all he had pulled out was an old boot. The second time, all he had pulled out was a broken pot full of mud. The third time he had cast his nets, and all he had pulled in was an old copper bottle. But there was something about the bottle that stopped the fisherman from hurling it back into the deeps. Perhaps it was the way the stopper glinted in the light. Or maybe it was the strange wax seal around the neck, highly decorated with strange markings. It might even have been the fact that the fisherman could have sworn he heard a faint noise coming from inside. In any case, something made the fisherman plunge his hand into his pocket for his penknife, slash the wax seal around the neck, and draw out the heavy stopper.

The fisherman turned the copper bottle upside down and shook it. All that came out was a trickle of dust as fine as sand . . . a trickle of dust that seemed to blow upwards with the wind, instead of falling down . . . a trickle of dust that became a wisp of smoke . . . a wisp of smoke that became a puff of mist . . . a puff of mist that

became a cloud
billowing overhead . . . a cloud
that formed huge feet and legs, and an
enormous body, and strong arms and hands –
and a massive, fierce, bald head with golden earrings
and a long moustache and cruel eyes. In other words, there
was a gigantic genie towering over him.

"Kneel before me, you spawn of a quivering jellyfish!" the
genie roared. "And prepare to meet your death!"

"What have I done?" the terrified fisherman begged, falling to
the sand. "I know the story of Aladdin and the genie of the lamp.
Haven't I set you free? Aren't you meant to grant me wishes?"

"You have indeed set me free," the gigantic genie bellowed,
"but it is FAR TOO LATE for wishes! For the first hundred years that
I was trapped inside that copper prison, I did indeed swear that I
would grant three wishes to anyone who set me free – no matter
how greedy they were. But no one helped me, and I grew
impatient. For the next two hundred years, I swore that I would
give never-ending riches to anyone who set me free. But no one
helped me, and I grew angry. For the next five hundred years, I

swore that I would give an entire kingdom to
anyone who set me free. But no one helped me – and I
grew furious. It was then that I swore that the very next
person I saw would taste my revenge. Now I have been trapped
inside that copper prison for TWO THOUSAND YEARS. And it is
you who will have the honour of receiving my punishment!"

The fisherman shuddered as the genie drew an enormous,
shining, curved sword from his belt. He began to think fast if there
were some way he could save himself . . .

To the genie's astonishment, the fisherman gave a friendly
wink. "Come on now," the fisherman smirked, "enough of this
fooling around. The way you appeared from nowhere like that was
really very impressive, but I should tell you that I simply don't
believe in magic."

"What do you mean, you don't believe in magic?" the genie
roared, his face as black as soot.

"Well, sorcerers and genies and spells – no one believes in all
that old rubbish nowadays," sniggered the fisherman, scornfully.

"Old rubbish!" blustered the genie, quite lost for words.

"So we've both had a bit of a laugh and a joke, haven't we?"
continued the fisherman, quite calmly. "Now, you just tell me where
you hid to make it look like you came out of the bottle, and I'll
congratulate you on your fantastic trick. Then you can tell me where
you're going to perform your conjuring show next time and I'll
promise to bring lots of gullible friends who'll pay good money to
watch you. And then we'll both shake hands on it and go home to
our wives. What do you say?"

"How dare you call me a fake!" boomed the raging genie, as
green smoke hissed out of his ears. "I'll show you that I'm real! I'll

show you that I'm the most terrifying genie that ever came out of a bottle – I'll prove it to you, by getting back into it right now!"

Suddenly the genie's massive face began to melt, his arms and legs began to blur, his huge body began to shimmer in the air. His features became formless and shifting like a great cloud of mist. Then the cloud narrowed into a spiral of smoke that funnelled round and down and round and down . . . and right into the neck of the bottle. As the very last wisp disappeared inside, the fisherman grabbed the heavy stopper and rammed it into the neck of the bottle as hard as he could.

"I shall never cast another net as long as I live," gasped the sweating fisherman, and he hurled the bottle as far as he could out into the ocean.

So if you're ever at the beach and you see a copper bottle bobbing about in the water or washed up on the shore, be very careful before you open it, won't you . . .

THE GIANT'S WIFE

an Irish legend

In the days when giants lived in the north of Ireland, Finn
McCoull was the biggest, strongest, most handsome of
them all – or so he thought. Finn could rip a pine tree out
of the ground with his bare hands. He could leap across a river in one
bound. He could split a boulder in half with one swish of his axe.

Now Finn had heard that there were clans of giants living in
Scotland who had tree trunk-throwing competitions and boulder-
carrying contests for fun. That sounded to him like great crack. So
Finn decided to build a road right across the sea, so he could walk
across to see these Scottish giants without getting his feet wet. Finn
pulled on his big black workboots, kissed his wife Oonagh goodbye,
and promised, "I'll be back in a week – ten days, tops." Then he
strode off over hills and forests to the coast.

Finn began to work hard, ripping rocks from the mountains and
throwing them into the sea until they piled up above the water and
began to form a road. However, he was only three days into the job
when a friend of his arrived at the seashore. "Finn, I don't mean to
worry you, to be sure," his friend said, "but there's gossip about a

strange giant who's on his way to your house to flatten you. Some say that he's leapt across the sea from Scotland without needing a boat or a bridge. People say he keeps a thunderbolt in his pocket. I've heard, too, that he has a magic little finger with as much strength in it as ten men put together!"

"Pah!" cried Finn, "I don't believe a word of it!" But secretly, he had begun to feel a little uneasy.

"One thing's for sure," his friend continued, "the stranger knows that everyone thinks you're the biggest, strongest, most handsome giant in all Ireland and he doesn't like it one little bit. He's made up his mind to find you and mince you into pieces!"

"We'll see about that!" bellowed Finn. "I'm going home right now to sit and wait for this pipsqueak of a giant, and if he dares to show his face at my front door, I'll stamp on him and squash him like an ant!" But even though Finn sounded brave, underneath it all he was really rather worried.

The minute that Finn arrived home, he sat down glumly at the kitchen table and told Oonagh all about the stories of the strange giant. "If it's true, he'll beat me into mashed potatoes!" Finn moaned.

"You men are always boasting about your muscles, but sometimes you should use your brains instead!" Oonagh laughed. "Now do as I say and leave everything else to me . . ."

Oonagh quickly found nine round flat stones and put them on a plate with a round flat oatcake, which she cleverly marked with a thumbprint so she could see which one it was. Meanwhile, Finn built an enormous baby's cradle and put it by the fireside, just as Oonagh had told him. Just then, Finn and Oonagh felt the ground begin to shake underneath them and a dark shadow fell across the house. "It's him! He's here!" panicked Finn, running to and fro in a tizzy.

"Whatever shall I do?" "Calm down!" urged Oonagh, handing her husband a bonnet and a nightdress. "Put these on and climb into the cradle!"

Finn was far too scared to argue, and soon he was dressed up like a baby and lying cuddled up in the crib. Oonagh shoved a huge bottle of milk into his mouth and went to answer the door.

"WHERE IS FINN McCOULL?" roared the massive giant who stood on the doorstep. He was certainly the biggest giant Oonagh had ever seen – and the ugliest! "WHEN I FIND HIM, I'M GOING TO RIP HIM TO SHREDS!" the giant bellowed.

"I'm afraid you've missed my husband," Oonagh smiled sweetly. "He's away at the coast, building a road across the sea to Scotland. He started this morning and he'll be finished by teatime. You can come in and wait for him if you like."

The massive giant growled something under his breath that may or may not have been "thank you".

Oonagh just laughed and gaily beckoned. "Well, you'd better

come in and have something to eat," she sang. "You'll need to get
your strength up if you're going to fight my Finn. I have to say you
look like a dwarf next to my fine husband!"

In the cradle, Finn's teeth began to chatter. What on earth was
his wife annoying the monster giant like that for?

"Have an oatcake," Oonagh offered the stranger politely,
putting one of the round, flat rocks on his plate.

The greedy giant crammed it into his mouth and took a huge
bite. "OW!" he roared, spitting bits of broken teeth all over the table.

"Oh dear, didn't you like it?" Oonagh fussed. "To be sure,
they're the baby's favourite!" She strode over to the cradle and gave
Finn the oatcake with the thumbprint. He munched on it happily.

The strange giant peered into the cradle and his eyes opened
wide. "That's Finn McCoull's baby?" he remarked, highly surprised.
"My, he's a whopper of a lad, isn't he?"

"Yes," sighed Oonagh, tickling her husband under the chin
while Finn cooed and gurgled as best he could. "He's got teeth all
ready, you know. Here, put your finger into his mouth and feel . . .
Go on."

Slowly, nervously, the giant put his magic little finger inside Finn's mouth.

CRUNCH! Finn bit down as hard as he could – right through the bone!

"AAAAAAARRRRRRRGGGGGHHHHHHHH!" roared the giant. "If Finn McCoull's baby is that powerful strong, I'm not hanging around to find out what Finn McCoull is like!" And he was out of the door and away over the hills before Finn McCoull could leap out of the cradle.

Finn McCoull never did finish his road across the sea. If you go to Ireland today, you can still see it poking out into the water, half-finished. He wanted nothing more than to stay at home and enjoy the rest of his days with his beautiful, clever wife. So that's exactly what he did.

THE THUNDER GOD GETS MARRIED

a Norse legend

Up in heaven, Thor the thunder god was furious. Someone had stolen his magic hammer. Thor's magic hammer was the terror of the gods. Whenever he threw it, it killed anything that it touched and it always returned to his hand. It was perhaps the most deadly weapon that the gods possessed to protect them against their enemies, the giants.

Now the raging Thor's roaring sounded like the clouds were clashing together. His face was so black with anger that it sent a dark shadow over the whole sky. As Thor grabbed blazing lightning bolts and hurled them through the clouds, the mischief-maker god, Loki, came nervously to see him. "I have good news, my angry friend," Loki explained. "I have used my cunning to find out that it is the giant Thrym who has stolen your hammer. He has agreed to give it back on one condition – that he has the most beautiful of all the goddesses, Freya, as his bride."

The thunder god's sulky face brightened a little and he charged off to find Freya straight away. "Put on your best dress, Freya!" Thor boomed, throwing open her wardrobe doors. "You have to marry the giant Thrym so I can get my magic hammer back."

Freya's eyes flickered with cold fire. "Excuse me, Thor," she said, calmly. "Would you care to repeat that?"

"You-have-to-marry-the-giant-Thrym-so-I-can-get-my-magic-hammer-back!" the impatient thunder god cried at top speed.

Freya stood glaring, her hands on her hips. "Firstly Thor, as the goddess of beauty I don't *have* to do anything."

Thor's face reddened.

"Secondly," Freya continued, "I wouldn't marry that ugly monster Thrym if he were the only creature left in the world."

The ashamed thunder god hung his head.

"Thirdly," Freya finished, "it's your problem, *you* sort it out."

"Sorry, Freya," Thor mumbled, shuffling about a bit. Then he turned and stormed back to Loki. The two gods sat down glumly and wracked their brains to come up with another way to get back the hammer.

"How about . . ." Thor started to suggest. Then he shook his head. "No, no good."

"What if . . ." Loki began. Then his face fell. "No, it would never work."

It looked as if Thor's magic hammer would have to stay in the land of the giants forever – until the god Heimdall had an idea.

"That's absolutely out of the question!" Thor thundered.

"Outrageous!" Loki squealed. "I'll never do it!"

"Well, you come up with another plan then," Heimdall laughed, knowing that there wasn't one.

That night, the giant Thrym was delighted to see a chariot with a bride and bridesmaid in it rumbling up to his castle steps. "It's Freya!" the gormless giant gasped with delight. "I shall gladly give back Thor's magic hammer in return for the most beautiful wife in the world!" The overjoyed giant commanded a magnificent wedding banquet to be prepared and his guests to be sent for at once.

But Thrym wouldn't have been so overjoyed if he could have seen what was underneath the veils of his bride and bridesmaid – the angry, highly-embarrassed faces of Thor and Loki! As it was, the giant was far too excited to notice how big and clumsy the bride and bridesmaid looked in their frilly dresses. Thrym didn't take in that the women had low, gruff voices and huge, hairy hands. And he hardly thought twice about the way that Freya swigged down two whole barrels of beer and devoured an entire roast ox.

When all the guests had eaten and drunk their fill, the beaming Thrym got to his feet to make a speech. "My wife and I," he began,

blushing bright red, "would like to thank you all for coming here today to celebrate this happy occasion with us. Freya has made me the luckiest being in the whole universe. And now, I will keep my word and give back the magic hammer I stole from that ugly thug of a thunder god."

There was a roll of drums as one of Thrym's servants brought in the magic hammer on a cushion. Thrym held it high in the air for his marvelling guests to admire, then with a grand flourish, he presented it to his bride.

"The ugly thug of a thunder god thanks you!" roared Thor, ripping off his veil and springing to his feet. And before Thrym and his guests could really take in the trick, they were lying dead on the floor and the wedding feast was unexpectedly over.

All the gods were truly relieved to have the magic hammer back in Thor's hands in heaven, where it belonged. But it was a long time before Thor and Loki could laugh with the other gods about how charming they both looked in a dress!

Royal Adventures

THE KING WITH DIRTY FEET
by Pomme Clayton

O nce upon a time there was a king. He lived in a hot, dusty village in India. He had everything he wanted and was very happy. But there was one thing that this king hated and that was bathtime.

Perhaps he was a bit like you?

This king had not washed for a week, he had not washed for a month, he had not washed for a whole year. He had begun to smell. He smelt underneath his arms, in between his toes, behind his ears and up his nose. He was the smelliest king there has ever been. His servants were all very polite about it, but nobody liked to be in the same room as him. Until one day the smell became too much for even the king himself, and he said rather sadly, "I think it is time I had a bath."

He walked slowly down to the river. The villagers whispered, "The king's going to have a bath!" and they rushed down to the river bank to get the best view.

Everyone fell silent when the king stepped into the cool, clear river water. When he called for the royal soap, a high cheer arose. He washed himself from top to bottom, scrubbed his hair and brushed his teeth. He played with his toy ducks and his little boat.

Then, at last, when he was quite clean, he called for the royal towel and stepped out of the river.

When he had finished drying himself he saw that his feet were covered in dust.

"Oh bother," he cried. "I forgot to wash them." So he stepped back into the water and soaped them well. But as soon as he stood on dry land his feet were dirty again.

"Oh my goodness," he said crossly. "I didn't wash them well enough. Bring me a scrubbing brush." The king scrubbed his feet until they shone. But still, when he stepped on the ground they were dirty.

This time the king was furious. He shouted for his servant, Gabu. Gabu came running and bowed before the king.

"Gabu," boomed the king, "the king has had a bath, the king is clean, but the earth is dirty. There is dust everywhere. You must clean the earth so there is no more dust and my feet stay clean."

"Yes, Your Majesty," replied Gabu.

"You have three days in which to rid the land of dust, and if you fail, do you know what will happen to you?" asked the king.

"No, Your Majesty."

"ZUT!" cried the king.

"ZUT?" said Gabu. "What is ZUT?"

"ZUT is the sound of your head being chopped off."

Gabu began to cry. "Don't waste time, Gabu. Rid the land of dust at once."

The king marched back to his palace.

"I must put my thinking cap on," said Gabu, and he put his head in his hands and began to think.

"When something is dirty, you brush it."

He asked all the villagers to help him. They took their brushes and brooms and ONE...TWO...THREE...

They all began to sweep–swish, swish, swish, swish, swish – all day long.

Until the dust rose up and filled the air in a thick, dark cloud. Everyone was coughing and spluttering and bumping into each other. The king choked, "Gabu, where are you? I asked you to rid the land of dust, not fill the air with dust. Gabu, you have two more days and ZUT!"

"Oh dear, oh dear," cried Gabu, and put his head in his hands and thought.

"When something is dirty you wash it."

He asked all the villagers to help him. They took their buckets to the well and filled them up to the brims with water and

ONE...TWO...THREE...

They all began to pour – sloosh, sloosh, sloosh, sloosh, sloosh – all day long.

There was so much water it spread across the land. It began to rise. Soon it was up to their ankles, their knees, their waists and then up to their chests.

"Swim everybody," cried Gabu.

The king climbed to the top of the highest mountain where the water lapped his toes and he sniffed, "Gabu, a-atchoo! Where are you?"

Gabu came swimming.

"Yes, Your Majesty?"

"Gabu, I asked you to rid the land of dust not turn our village into a swimming pool. You have one more day and ZUT!"

"Oh dear, oh dear, I have run out of ideas," cried Gabu. The water trickled away and Gabu put his head in his hands and thought.

"I could put the king in an iron room with no windows or doors, chinks or cracks, then no speck of dust would creep in. But I don't think he would like that. Oh, if only I could cover up all the dust with a carpet." Then Gabu had a marvellous idea.

"Of course, why didn't I think of this before? Everyone has a needle and thread and a little piece of leather. Leather is tough, we will cover the land with leather."

He asked all the villages to help him.  Needles were threaded and knots were tied and ONE...TWO...THREE...

They all began to sew – stitch, stitch, stitch, stitch, stitch – all day long.

Then the huge piece of leather was spread across the land and it fitted perfectly. It stretched from the school to the well, from the temple to the palace, and all the way down to the river.

"We've done it," cried Gabu. "I will go and tell the king." Gabu knocked on the palace door.

"We are ready, Your Majesty."

The king poked his head carefully around the door not knowing what to expect. Then a little smile twitched at the corner of his mouth. The ground looked clean, very clean indeed. He put one foot on the leather and it was spotless. The king walked across the leather.

"This is splendid, comfortable, clean. Well done, Gabu. Well done."

The king turned to the villagers to thank them.

Suddenly, out of the crowd stepped a little old man with a long white beard and a bent back. Everyone had quite forgotten him. He bowed low before the king and spoke in a very quiet voice.

"Your Majesty, how will anything be able to grow now that the land is covered with leather? The grass will not be able to push its way through. There will no vegetables or flowers and no new trees. The animals will be hungry and there will be nothing for us to eat."

Now everyone was listening.

"Your Majesty, you know you don't have to cover the land with leather to keep your feet clean. It is really quite simple."

The old man took out of his pocket a large pair of scissors. He bent down and began to cut the leather very carefully all around the king's feet. Then he took two laces from his pockets and tied each piece of leather to the king's feet. Then he pulled back the leather that covered the earth and said, "Try them,

Your Majesty."

The king looked down at his feet covered in leather and frowned. He had never seen anything like it. He put one foot forward.

"Mmm, very good!" he exclaimed. He took another step.

"This is splendid, comfortable, clean and the grass can grow!"

Then the king walked, then he ran and then he jumped.

"Hooray," he cried. "I can walk here, and here, and here. I can walk anywhere and my feet will always be clean."

What was the king wearing on his feet?

That's right, he was wearing SHOES!

They were the first pair of shoes ever to be made, and people have been wearing them ever since.

SNIP, SNAP, SNOUT, MY STORY IS OUT!

THE EMPEROR'S NEW CLOTHES

retold from the original tale by Hans Christian Andersen

There was once an emperor who loved new clothes above everything else. Designers, tailors, clothmakers, dyers, and specialists in all sorts of needlework travelled to his city from all over the world. Anyone who could suggest flashy, fancy new outfits for the emperor was always very welcome at the palace.

One day, it was the turn of two weavers to be ushered into the emperor's dressing room. The emperor, his butler and all his Officers of the Royal Wardrobe, gasped with amazement as they listened to them describe their work. "We have created a special type of fabric that is so light and airy the wearer cannot feel it is there," the first weaver announced.

"Our samples are top secret, which is why we have not been able to bring any to show you," the second weaver explained.

"However we can assure you that not only are our designs and patterns exquisitely beautiful," said the first weaver, "but the fabric has the unique advantage that it is completely invisible to anyone who is not worthy of his job —"

"— or who is just plain stupid!" laughed the second weaver, and the emperor and all his courtiers gasped and chuckled along.

"We would be honoured if you would like to order the very first suit of clothes made out of this extraordinary fabric, your imperial majesty," said the first weaver, bowing low.

The emperor clapped his hands with delight. "I'd like to place an order right away!" he commanded, and he gave the two weavers a large sum of money so that they could buy the rare, expensive materials they needed and begin their work without delay.

The weavers set up their looms in the palace studio and got going right away. News of the strange cloth spread round the city like wildfire and soon everyone was talking about it. But the weavers worked behind closed doors and no one got even a glimpse of what they were doing. Still, day and night everyone heard the looms clicking and the shuttles flying, and work on the magical cloth seemed to be progressing well.

As the days went on, the emperor began to feel rather uneasy about seeing the cloth for the first time. *Imagine if I can't see the fabric myself!* he thought to himself. *How dreadfully embarrassing that would be!* The worried emperor decided to send his trusted old butler to see how the weavers were getting on. He was sure that his butler was both fit for his job and very wise, and would be sure to see the wonderful material.

The weavers bowed low and ushered the butler into the studio. But the butler couldn't see anything at all. *Heavens above!* the butler thought to himself. *Those looms look totally bare to me! I must either be a very bad butler, or else I'm an idiot. No one must ever find out . . .* So he praised the material that he could not see, told the king that the

weavers' work was indeed
magnificent, and everyone in
the city heard that the cloth
was truly unbelieveable!

Soon afterwards, the weavers
sent word to the emperor that
they needed more money to buy
essential items for the work. The
emperor had been so delighted with
the butler's report that he sent them
twice as much money as before.

The emperor was more excited
than ever. "I'm going to have the
most amazing suit of clothes in the world!" he
giggled to himself ten times a day.

Eventually, just as the impatient emperor thought he was going
to explode with waiting, the weavers announced their work was
finished. They went to the dressing room to present the material to
the emperor amid fanfares of trumpets. "Is the cloth not beautiful
beyond all imagining?" the weavers sighed.

The emperor smiled a wide smile, trying to hide his horror. All
that the weavers appeared to be holding up before him was thin air.
The emperor's worst fear had come true – to him the cloth was
invisible! *I cannot be thought to be a fool or not worthy to be ruler,* the
despairing emperor thought. So he beamed and leant forwards and
inspected the air. "Wonderful! Splendid! Magnificent!" he cried, and
his butler and all the Officers of the Royal Wardrobe nodded and
cried out compliments. None of them could see anything either, but
they weren't about to risk losing their jobs by admitting it.

So the weavers got out their tape measures and their scissors and they set about cutting the thin air (or so it seemed) into a pattern. All night long they sewed with needles which appeared to have no thread, and in the morning they announced that the emperor's new clothes were ready. "Now if your imperial majesty would care to disrobe, we will dress you in the amazing garments."

The emperor swallowed hard and took off all his clothes. The weavers helped him on with the underpants and trousers and shirt and jacket that he couldn't see. "Aren't they lighter than cobwebs?" they sighed. The emperor spluttered his agreement. He couldn't feel that he had any clothes on at all.

The emperor stood back and looked at himself in the mirror. According to what he saw, he didn't have a stitch on! But he turned this way and that, pretending to admire himself. And the butler and all the Officers of the Royal Wardrobe cried out, "How wonderfully the new clothes fit you, sire!" and "We have never seen the like of the amazing colours!" and "The design is a work of genius!" – even though it looked to them as if the emperor was as naked as the day he was born.

Everyone else can see my new suit except me, the emperor thought to himself glumly. And he walked out of the palace to parade before the people in his marvellous new clothes.

The streets were lined with hundreds of men and women who *ooohed!* and *aaaahed!* over the emperor's invisible new clothes – for none of them wanted to admit that they couldn't see them.

Suddenly, a little boy's shrill voice rose over the applause of the crowd. "But the emperor has nothing on!" the child shouted. "Nothing on at all!" Suddenly there was a stunned silence and the little boy found that hundreds of pairs of eyes were staring at him. Then someone sniggered . . . someone else tried to stifle a giggle . . .

another person guffawed and snorted . . . and the whole crowd burst out into uncontrollable peals of laughter.

The emperor's face turned as red as a ripe tomato. "I am indeed a fool!" he murmured. "I have been swindled by two tricksters!" He ran back to the palace as fast as his short, naked legs could carry him – but the clever (and now very rich) weavers were long gone!

THE LITTLE MERMAID

retold from the original tale by Hans Christian Andersen

Far, far out in the ocean, the water is as blue as cornflowers and deeper than the tallest mountain. It is there that the sea-people live, and in the very deepest waters lies the Sea King's palace of coral and mother-of-pearl. The Sea King's beloved wife had died, so his mother, the old queen, took care of his six beautiful mermaid daughters. All day long, the princesses sang and danced, swimming in and out of the pillars and halls of the palace. Sometimes shy, brightly coloured fish swam up to eat out of their hands. And at other times, each would tend the little garden that she cared for in the royal grounds. Each mermaid princess gave her garden its own particular style and design: one was shaped like a whale; another had a rockery of shells; yet another had flowerbeds where the sea-horses came to graze. But the youngest mermaid's garden was shaped like the sun that shone on the world above the sea, and the flowers that grew there blazed red and orange and yellow like the sunlight.

The little mermaid had never been up to the ocean's surface and seen the upper world, for the princesses were only allowed to do so when they reached fifteen years old. But the little mermaid longed for that day to come. She loved to hear the stories her grandmother told of people and ships and cities and animals and meadows and forests and the like. And many a night the little mermaid stood at her open chamber window, peering up at the watery reflections of the moon and the stars and the dark shapes of ships as they passed like clouds above her.

When each of her sisters came of age, the little mermaid begged them eagerly to tell her everything they had seen. Then at last, she turned fifteen and it was her turn to see the upper world for herself.

The little mermaid thought it was more beautiful than she had ever imagined. Her head broke through the foam when the sun had just gone down and the clouds looked as if they were on fire with red and gold. The sound of music and singing was coming from a tall-masted ship bedecked all about with coloured flags and banners. Suddenly rockets zoomed up from it into the sky which exploded into stars that fell glittering all around her – the little mermaid had never seen fireworks before. When she was lifted up on the swell of the sea, she saw onto the ship's magnificent deck and understood the reason for the wonderful celebrations: it was the birthday party of a prince, more handsome than any merman she had ever seen.

As the little mermaid gazed with delight at the prince and his ship, she heard a familiar rumbling stirring deep within the sea. A storm was coming! All at once the sky darkened. Sheets of rain lashed the ship. The waves towered into mountains that hurled the ship upwards and sent it crashing down towards the depths. The little mermaid saw with alarm that the ship wouldn't be able to hold out against the might of the weather and the ocean, and she ducked under the waves as wooden planks and other pieces of the ship came flying out of the darkness at her head. Through the murky waters, the little mermaid was horrified to see human bodies come floating down around her – and among them was her beautiful prince, choking and gasping for air.

The little mermaid shot through the water and clutched him close to her, and began swimming up to the light until his head was above water. The little mermaid hauled the exhausted prince to the shore and let the waves wash him onto the sand, and she stayed in the foam and watched him until the storm had died away and the morning sunlight came streaming warmly through the clouds. Then she saw the green hills for the first time and heard the peal of bells, and she saw a group of young girls come skipping out of a white building with a cross on the top. One of the girls noticed the prince where he lay. She ran to him and laid his head in her lap, and slowly the prince opened his eyes. He looked up at the girl and smiled, and the little mermaid turned away sadly, for she knew the prince thought it was that girl who had rescued him. Down, down, down, the little mermaid dived into the deeps – and her heart ached all the way back to her father's palace.

From that moment on, the little mermaid was thoughtful and sad. She longed to see her handsome prince again, to tell him that she loved him and wanted to be with him forever. She wanted to be human more than anything else in the whole world. There was only one thing she could do: make the dangerous journey to the cold, dark depths of the ocean to see the Water-Witch.

The Water-Witch's lair was set about with the skeletons of humans she had drowned and the remains of ships she had wrecked. The little mermaid trembled with fear as she explained why she had come.

"What you long for is extremely difficult to give," the Water-Witch cackled. "I can make your tail disappear and give you legs so that you can walk about with the humans in the world above. But every step you take will be as painful as if you are treading on knives. And I cannot make your prince fall in love with you. It is up to you, and you alone, to do that. If your prince marries another, the morning afterwards your heart will break and you will turn to foam on the water."

The little mermaid shuddered, but she bade the Water-Witch continue.

"The price for such strong magic is very high," spat the witch. "Once I have given you legs, there is no changing your mind. You will never be able to return to the sea as a mermaid to see your family . . . And there is one more thing. I cannot mix the potion you need unless you give me your voice."

The little mermaid longed so badly for her prince and for a human soul that she whispered, "So be it." The words were the last sounds she ever uttered. For then the Water-Witch took the little mermaid's voice and brewed up an evil-smelling potion for her in exchange.

The little mermaid felt as if her heart would break with grief as she swam back past her father's palace, leaving her sleeping family for

the world above. She splashed onto the sand, half-choking through
her tears and half-gasping for air, and looked at her beautiful silvery
fishtail for the last time. Then the little mermaid raised the witch's
brew to her lips and drank deeply. At once pain wracked her body
and she fell into a dead faint . . .

The little mermaid awoke to find her handsome prince standing
over her, looking worried. "Are you all right?" he asked, but the little
mermaid couldn't reply. Instead, she smiled as she looked down at
her body and saw that she had the prettiest pair of legs she could
have wished for. Falteringly, she stood up for the very first time. The
little mermaid put out her foot – and it was true, each step was like
treading on knives. But soon she was dancing and running and
skipping along the beach for joy, and the prince was utterly
enchanted.

The prince took his new little friend back to the palace and
dressed her in fine robes of silk and satin. He didn't seem to mind
that she was dumb, and kept her by his side at all times, calling her
"my beautiful little foundling".

Yet although the little mermaid was happier than she had ever
dreamed was possible, there was a sadness in her
eyes and a heaviness in her heart. Each night, she
would creep out of the palace and go down to
the seashore. Sometimes she saw her sisters
way out among the surf, and they would
sing to her sadly as they floated on the
waves. Once, she even thought she
glimpsed the golden crowns of her father
and grandmother – but perhaps it was just the
moonlight glinting on the water.

Eventually a day came when the prince led the little mermaid onto a fine ship just like the one from which she had rescued him. They sailed for a night and a day, and all the time the little mermaid longed to leap into the waves and dive down to see her family far below. The ship finally arrived in the harbour of a neighbouring kingdom, and all the people lined the streets to meet them, waving flags and cheering. "See how they welcome me," the prince whispered to the little mermaid. "For today I am going to marry their princess."

The little mermaid felt as if someone had grabbed her heart with icy fingers. Surely it couldn't be true? But when the prince's bride came running down the palace steps to meet him, the little mermaid understood. It was the girl who had found him on the beach; the girl whom the prince thought had saved him from the sea; the girl whom the prince thought was the little mermaid.

That afternoon, the little mermaid stood in church dressed in silk and gold, holding the bride's train. And all the way back to the ship, she cried silent, dry tears.

That night, as the splendid ship floated on the waves, there were flags and fireworks and music and dancing – and the little mermaid felt no more a part of the celebrations than she had when she had watched the prince's birthday party from afar.

The little mermaid stood on the deck all night and listened to the sighing of the sea. She felt the warm night wind on her face and her hair floated in the damp sea mists. When the first rays of the dawn lit up the horizon, the little mermaid prepared herself to dissolve into foam on the waves. But instead, she saw transparent beings of light flying to her through the air. They lifted her up on their wings and soared off into the sky, and the little mermaid found that she was one of them. "We are the daughters of the air," the beautiful beings explained. "We do not have an immortal soul, but if we perform enough acts of goodness and kindness, we will one day win one for ourselves. And this is your reward for the suffering you have endured."

The little mermaid raised her hands towards the sun and the tears in her eyes were tears of joy. She looked down upon the prince and his bride on their ship. They were searching for her sadly in the water, thinking she had fallen overboard. But the little mermaid didn't stay to watch them for long. She blew them a kiss and flew onwards with the daughters of the air.

THE GOLDEN TOUCH

a myth from Ancient Greece

There was once a king called Midas who loved gold more than anything in the world. Each day, he spent hour after hour in his treasure house, running his hands through his sacks of gold coins, admiring his golden jars and statues, and holding up his golden jewellery to the light to watch it gleam and shine. Midas thought that the precious metal was a much more delightful colour than the emerald green of the grass or the sapphire blue of the sea. He thought it was far more beautiful than the gold of waving fields of wheat, the gold of his wife's hair – even the gold of sunshine.

The king once helped the god Dionysus by taking care of one of his friends who was lost. Dionysus was very grateful and insisted, "Let me repay you for your kindness by granting you a wish! Now think hard . . . Make it something good! . . . Whatever you like . . ."

Midas knew exactly what he wanted. "I wish for everything I touch to turn to gold!" he declared.

"Are you sure about that?" Dionysus asked. "Are you quite, quite sure?"

"What could be better?" cried Midas, delightedly.

"Very well then," sighed the god. "It is done."

Midas couldn't wait to try out his new powers. He hurried over to a tree and snapped off a twig. Unbelievable! It immediately grew heavy and bright. It had turned to solid gold. Joyfully, Midas rushed around touching everything in his royal garden. Soon the apples hung on the trees like golden baubles. The flowers hardened into gold sculptures. The fountain froze into a spray of golden glitter and the grass solidified into a gold pavement.

"How wonderful!" laughed Midas, clapping his hands. "Now for my palace!" and he picked up his robes and ran inside. By the time Midas reached the cool of his great chamber, his clothes had stiffened into a fabric woven from pure gold thread. "Ooof!" puffed Midas. "That's a little heavy!" The weight of his golden clothes were dragging him down, slowing him up and making his shoulders ache. *Still*, thought Midas, *that's a minor botheration compared to how beautiful my robes now look!* He set off through the halls and corridors, touching pillars, pictures, doors, furniture, floors . . . until everything glowed gold.

Phew! It was hungry, thirsty work! Midas sank into one of his new golden chairs at his new golden dining table and called for his servants to bring him his lunch. He wriggled about a bit on his rock hard seat, but couldn't get comfy. "Never mind!" said Midas to himself, as the servants brought in platter after platter of delicious food. "I don't know any other king who is rich enough to eat off gold plates!" And he touched each serving dish and bowl and saw them gleam.

"Amazing!" Midas whooped, and licking his lips, he reached for a juicy chicken leg. "OWWW!" he yelled, biting down on hard metal and breaking a tooth. He reached for a goblet of wine and took a gulp. "AAARRGH!" Midas roared, as the mouthful of gold got stuck in his throat. The king pushed his chair back, spitting out the hunk of treasure.

"Oh, no!" the king moaned. Suddenly he realised what the god Dionysus had been trying to warn him about. "I'm going to have a whole kingdom full of gold, but I'm not going to be able to eat or drink anything!"

At that very moment, Midas's golden doors swung open and his little daughter came running towards him. Midas backed away in horror – but it was too late. "Daddy!" the little girl cried, flinging her arms happily around him. Suddenly the king's beloved daughter was no more than a lifeless statue. Midas howled with misery and huge tears began to stream from his eyes. "I would gladly give away every piece of gold that I own to have my little girl back again," he wailed. "How foolish I have been! There must be some way to take back my wish!"

Desperately trying not to touch anything else, Midas hurried to Dionysus and begged him to undo his magic. "Go and wash in the River Pactolus," the god instructed him. As soon as the king had done so, he was hugely relieved to find that his golden touch was gone. All the things Midas had turned into gold were back to normal – including his beautiful little daughter. After that, if the king had had his way, he would never have looked at another nugget of gold as long as he lived. But the god Dionysus turned the sandy bed of the River Pactolus gold for ever more, so that every time Midas walked along its banks, he would remember his greedy mistake.

THE NUTCRACKER PRINCE

retold from the original tale by Ernst Hoffmann

r Drosselmeier was an old man with a secret. In his youth, he had been the most nimble-fingered, highly skilled craftsman in the entire royal court. Dr Drosselmeier had made clocks that were mechanical wonders. Some chimed with a hundred tinkling bells. Others were decorated with tiny musicians that danced and played their instruments as they struck the hour. Some even had secret doors, out of which little birds fluttered and flew around the room, chirruping the passing minutes. Yes, Dr Drosselmeier's clocks had been the talk of the palace. But the most amazing thing he had ever made was a mouse-trap.

Dr Drosselmeier had invented a brilliant clockwork trap that caught mice in their hundreds, twenty-four hours a day. Everyone in the palace had been delighted – except for the Mouse King. He too had lived in the palace with his subjects. Now, he was forced to leave and find another home, and he was furious about it. The Mouse King knew powerful magic and he took his revenge on Dr Drosselmeier by turning his nephew into an ugly, wooden doll.

The doll wore a painted soldier's uniform and it had a prince's crown

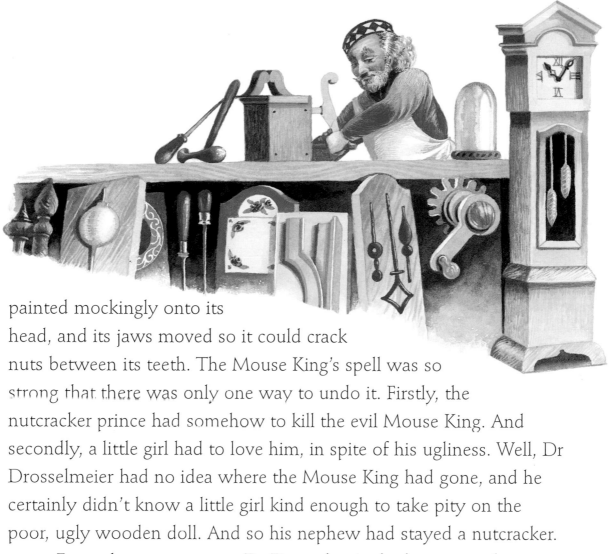

painted mockingly onto its
head, and its jaws moved so it could crack
nuts between its teeth. The Mouse King's spell was so
strong that there was only one way to undo it. Firstly, the
nutcracker prince had somehow to kill the evil Mouse King. And
secondly, a little girl had to love him, in spite of his ugliness. Well, Dr
Drosselmeier had no idea where the Mouse King had gone, and he
certainly didn't know a little girl kind enough to take pity on the
poor, ugly wooden doll. And so his nephew had stayed a nutcracker.

From that moment on, Dr Drosselmeier had never made
another clock. He lost all heart for mechanical things and so he lost
his job at the palace, too. Dr Drosselmeier blamed himself entirely for
his nephew's dreadful disappearance and he had never breathed a
word of what had happened to anyone. But ever since, he had been
trying to find a way to break the Mouse King's spell . . . and at last,
he thought he had.

Dr Drosselmeier's goddaughter, Clara, had grown into the
kindest little girl anyone could wish to meet. If any little girl was
going to take pity on the stiff, glaring nutcracker prince, it would
be Clara.

Now it was Christmas Eve, and Dr Drosselmeier had arrived at Clara's house trembling with excitement. He wasn't excited because there was a party going on with games and music and dancing. No, Dr Drosselmeier was excited because tonight was the night he hoped the evil magic would be undone and his nephew would return to life.

While the party guests talked and joked and laughed together, Dr Drosselmeier set about emptying the huge bag he had brought with him. It was filled with gingerbread and shortcake, candy walking sticks and sugar pigs, nuts and bon bons, nougat and humbugs . . . High and low, in every corner of the room, Dr Drosselmeier heaped piles of all the Mouse King's favourite things to eat. *That should tempt him out from wherever he's hiding,* thought Dr Drosselmeier, determinedly.

Then it was time to give Clara her Christmas present. The little girl's eyes opened wide with excitement as she stripped off the sparkly paper. But her face suddenly fell as she saw the ugly nutcracker prince. Then, gently, Clara stroked the doll's face. He wasn't cute, he wasn't cuddly – he wasn't even new! But that was exactly why Clara decided she loved him. She couldn't bear to think of leaving him all alone, laughed at and unloved – especially at Christmas time. Clara clutched the nutcracker prince close to her and hugged him tight. And Dr Drosselmeier slipped away from the party, his heart light with hope . . .

When the party was over and it was bedtime at last, Clara tucked the wooden doll up next to her. "I love you," she whispered, just before she fell asleep. "I'll look after you always." And that night, Clara had a very strange dream. She dreamt that the nutcracker prince woke up beside her. He smiled at Clara and held her hand, and led her downstairs. There was scuffling and squeaking coming from the drawing room, and when Clara peeped around the door she saw a terrible sight. There were mice everywhere! They were climbing all over Dr Drosselmeier's goodies, fighting and biting each other to get at the sweets. And worst of all, a horrible seven-headed mouse was standing in the middle of the carpet, cackling with glee at all the arguing and the mess. The seven-headed mouse wore seven golden crowns and Clara could tell at once that he must be the king of the evil creatures.

Very bravely, the nutcracker prince charged at the gruesome Mouse King with a sword glinting in his hand and began to fight furiously. But he was completely outnumbered. The mice swarmed to their king's defence. They dragged the nutcracker prince to the ground and he disappeared under a thousand biting, clawing bodies. Just as the Mouse King threw back his head and began to laugh, Clara tore her slipper off her foot and threw it at him with all her might. WHAM! It hit the Mouse King on four of his seven horrible heads. He staggered to and fro for a second, and then collapsed dead to the floor.

As soon as the mice saw that their leader was no more, their courage deserted them. They hurried to scoop up his body and then they were gone, streaming off through cracks in the wall, holes in the skirting and gaps in the floorboards.

The nutcracker prince ran to Clara and kissed her. "Thank you for all you have done for me," he whispered, and there were tears sparkling in his painted eyes. "Let me repay you by taking you on a wonderful journey to my kingdom, the realm of sweets . . ."

It was the most wonderful dream Clara had ever had. She travelled through forests made of barley sugar, crossed rivers that ran with lemonade, picked flowers of sherbert, walked on paths of chocolate, and visited the nutcracker prince's gingerbread castle. In fact, Clara was very sorry to be woken up – even though it was Christmas Day itself! She hugged the wooden doll and told him, "You're the best present I've ever had," and she could have sworn that his smile was even broader than usual.

Meanwhile, across the city, Dr Drosselmeier had also woken up to find the best present he'd ever had. There sprawled underneath his Christmas tree, sleeping an exhausted but peaceful sleep, was his brave, handsome nephew . . .

THE SWORD IN THE STONE
a Celtic legend

The blacksmith's anvil had suddenly appeared in the courtyard of the cathedral on Christmas morning. No one knew how it had got there. The anvil had a sword stuck into it and stood on a huge stone. Words were carved right round it which read: *Whoever pulls out this sword is the rightful king of the Britons.*

Many a proud lord had stepped up and tried to pull the sword out of the mysterious anvil. But even though they had heaved and sweated and grunted and pulled and pulled and pulled, all of them had walked away disappointed. Now almost a week had passed. It was time for the New Year's Eve jousting festival, and still the anvil stood on the stone in the courtyard with the sword sticking out of it.

Every year, bold knights came to the capital city from all over the kingdom to ride against each other in the New Year's Eve jousting festival and show off how brave they were. This year, Sir Ector's son, Sir Kay, would joust for the very first time. Sir Ector's younger son, Arthur, was going along too, as Sir Kay's squire. Sir Ector and his sons lived in the very furthest corner of the kingdom – so far away from the capital city that news of the strange anvil hadn't even reached them. It took them three days of hard riding until they saw the towering cathedral spire and the bright fluttering flags of the jousting field in the distance. Then a dreadful thing happened. Sir Kay put his hand down by his side to pat his trusty sword – and there was nothing there. "My sword!" Sir Kay gasped. "It's gone!"

Arthur turned quite pale with horror. It was a squire's job to make sure that a knight was properly equipped. "We must have left it at the lodging house we stayed at last night," he groaned. "Don't worry, Kay. I'll dash back and fetch it." Before anyone could argue, Arthur had wheeled his horse around and was galloping at full tilt back down the road. There wasn't a second to lose.

But when Arthur arrived back at the lodging house, there wasn't a sign of Sir Kay's sword anywhere. Arthur raced his horse back to the city wondering how on earth he was going to break the bad news to his brother. He was very nearly at the jousting field when he galloped past the cathedral courtyard and saw the sword sticking out of the magical anvil on the stone. Arthur reined in his panting horse at once and looked all around him. There was no one about; everyone was at the jousting competition. It certainly didn't look as if the sword would be missed if he borrowed it for a while. "I promise I'll bring it back later," Arthur muttered out loud to no one in particular. He dashed over the snow, jumped up onto the stone and grasped the sword. It slid out of the anvil as easily as a needle pulls through cloth. "Gadzooks!" Arthur breathed, as he gazed at the mighty, jewelled blade in his hands. "This is the most magnificent weapon I have ever seen!" Then he remembered that the competition was about to begin. He sprinted back to his horse, leapt into the saddle, and arrived at the jousting field just as the first fanfares were being trumpeted.

Sir Kay was astonished at the superb weapon that his younger brother handed him. He and his father had just heard all about the mysterious anvil from the other knights at the jousting competition, and he realised at once where the strange sword must have come from. "See, father!" he cried over the crowds, brandishing the sword over his head. "I must be the new king of the Britons!"

Sir Ector came running at once and gasped at the magnificent weapon in Kay's hands. "How have you got this?" he demanded.

Kay's face fell. "Arthur brought it to me," he mumbled.

Sir Ector's face was grave. "Who pulled this out of the stone and gave it to you?" he quizzed Arthur.

"N-n-o one," stammered Arthur. Quite a few people had gathered around by now, pointing and shouting and staring, and suddenly he felt very nervous. "I pulled it out of the stone myself. I was going to put it back when Kay had finished with it, honest!"

Sir Ector led Arthur back to the cathedral and into the courtyard, with a huge and excited crowd following hot on their heels. "Put the sword back where you found it, son," he told Arthur.

"All right," shrugged Arthur. He climbed onto the stone and thrust the sword back into the anvil.

First, Sir Ector himself tried to pull it out. Then Sir Kay heaved at it with all his might. The sword didn't budge an inch.

"Now show us how you did it, son," said Sir Ector, his voice trembling slightly.

Everyone held their breath as Arthur stepped up to the anvil. As he pulled the sword out effortlessly, the cheer that went up could be heard all over the capital city and beyond.

And that is how a young boy called Arthur, who wasn't even a knight, was crowned king of the Britons and eventually became the greatest of all the heroes who ever lived in the Celtic lands.

RICKY WITH THE TUFT

retold from the original story by Charles Perrault

aaarrggh!" cried the queen, as she saw her newborn son for the first time. "Surely this baby can't be mine! He's hideously ugly!"

The fairy midwife sighed. It was true. The tiny face of the queen's new baby boy was swamped by a huge red nose. He was cross-eyed and his shoulders were humped. One of his legs was much shorter than the other. And to top it all, the baby was totally bald except for a single tuft of hair sticking up in the middle of his head. "Never mind your little boy's looks, your majesty," the fairy midwife comforted the queen. "I promise that your son will grow up to be far more intelligent, witty and charming than other people, and everyone will love him for it. What's more, I'm going to give him a gift. I'm going to give him the power to make the girl he falls in love with as intelligent as he is, so he won't ever get bored with her company . . . Now, what are you going to call your special little son?"

"Ricky . . ." the queen decided, making up her mind that she loved her son after all. "He's my little Ricky with the Tuft."

Not long afterwards, the queen of a neighbouring kingdom

gave birth to twin daughters. The first tiny girl to be born was so perfect that the queen at first thought she was looking at a little angel from heaven. But the second baby was as ugly as her elder sister was beautiful.

"Oh dear," said the fairy midwife – the same one who had helped at the birth of Ricky with the Tuft. "I have to tell you that your elder daughter will grow up to be incrediby stupid . . . However, there is some comfort. Your younger daughter will stay ugly, but she will be so clever that no one will even notice."

The queen was relieved that her younger daughter's fate seemed to be taken care of, but she was very worried about her elder daughter. "Can't we somehow give the elder one some of the younger one's intelligence?" the queen suggested.

"I'm afraid that's beyond my powers," the fairy midwife replied. "However, what I can do for her is to make her more beautiful than any girl in the world. What's more, I'll also give her a gift. The boy she falls in love with will become as beautiful as she is, so she'll never tire of looking at him."

Sixteen or so years passed, and the two princesses grew up exactly as the fairy midwife had said they would. Strangers were at first entranced by the beauty of the elder princess. However, they would soon creep away because trying to make conversation with her was as difficult as digging a field with a spoon. The strangers would then turn to the younger princess and be captivated by her intelligent and entertaining chat. Everyone totally forgot how plain and ungainly the princess was after only five minutes in her enchanting company.

Unfortunately, the beautiful elder sister knew very well that she was exceedingly stupid and embarrassing. She often stole away into the woods to be on her own – and it was on one of these lonely walks that she first encountered Ricky with the Tuft.

It wasn't an accident that the princess and the prince came to meet each other. Ricky with the Tuft had fallen desperately in love with the pictures of the princess that were for sale in all the shops. After collecting every single one, sticking them all over his bedroom walls, and gazing at them adoringly for hours on end, Ricky with the Tuft had decided that he wanted to marry the real thing. He had set off determined to find her.

"My lady, I feel as if I have been looking for you all my life," sighed Ricky with the Tuft, bowing low to the princess.

The princess just shrugged, as she couldn't think of anything to

say to the remarkably ugly prince who stood before her.

"I have never seen a girl as beautiful as you," admitted Ricky with the Tuft. "And as I should know more than most, beauty is an important blessing that shouldn't be taken for granted."

The sad princess blurted out, "I would much rather be as ugly as you are, if only I could be a little less stupid!"

Luckily, Ricky with the Tuft wasn't offended. "I have the perfect solution," he smiled. "I love you with all my heart, and if you will only consent to be my wife, you will become as wise and witty as you could ever wish to be."

The princess wasn't sure if she understood or not what the ugly prince was saying. She stood gaping open-mouthed.

"I can see you are a little taken aback by the suddenness of my proposal," said Ricky with the Tuft, kindly. "So I will give you a whole year to get used to the idea."

The princess said nothing to disagree, and so Ricky with the Tuft trotted off home, his heart full to bursting with happiness.

From that moment on, the princess discovered that she was as intelligent and entertaining as she was beautiful. The news spread rapidly, and princes and lords and earls came from kingdoms far and wide to seek her hand in marriage. Of course, in all the excitement, the princess quite forgot about Ricky with the Tuft. Her mind was completely taken up with one big worry. The princess thought each suitor very handsome in his own way, but now that she herself was so clever, she found them all extremely boring! "How can I marry a man whose conversation sends me to sleep within five minutes?" she sighed wistfully.

One day, the princess decided to wander alone into the woods to think the problem over. She hadn't been gone long when she came

across a hundred servants preparing a banquet among the trees. They were hanging flags and balloons and coloured lanterns in the branches; they were scurrying to and fro in a vast outdoor kitchen, cooking a delicious feast; they were setting up a dance floor and a bandstand, and laying thousands of tables and chairs – all beautifully decked with flowers. "Whatever is going on?" the astounded princess asked one of the servants. She had attended many wonderful balls, but had never been to one on such a grand, gorgeous scale. "The person giving this banquet must have a very important reason to throw such a wonderful party."

"Tomorrow our master, Ricky with the Tuft, is getting married," the breathless servant replied. "He loves his bride with all his heart and is throwing the best wedding feast ever!"

The princess gasped as she suddenly remembered the squinting, limping, hunchbacked prince with the huge nose and the strange tuft of hair, whom she had met exactly a year before. *I gave him the impression I would marry him!* she thought in horror.

The princess suddenly saw Ricky with the Tuft himself heading through the trees towards her. "Good afternoon, my darling," he cried. "I have kept my word and have come to see how you feel about marrying me now."

The princess hung her head in shame. "There is no doubt in my mind that you are the kindest, most honourable, most intelligent person in the world," she sobbed. "I would love to be with you forever – but I can't! I am deeply sorry that I can never marry you, for I can't get over your terrible ugliness!"

To the princess's amazement, Ricky with the Tuft laughed out loud. "Well, I do believe that you've fallen in love with me after all," he cried. And when the princess looked up, she saw that Ricky with the Tuft had become as handsome as she herself was beautiful. "Didn't you know you had the power to do that?" the prince beamed.

The princess fell into his arms, and the very next day, she and her prince had the best wedding feast ever - just as Ricky with the Tuft had wanted.

THE HAPPY PRINCE

retold from the original tale by Oscar Wilde

The statue of the Happy Prince stood high up above the city on a tall column. He glittered in the sunlight, for he was painted all over in gold leaf and had a glowing ruby set into his sword hilt and two sparkling sapphires for eyes. The people of the city often looked up at the Happy Prince and sighed, for they admired his beauty and envied his contented smile.

One evening, a little swallow came fluttering through the skies and landed between the prince's golden feet. It was well past the end of the summer and the wind had grown chill. The swallow's friends had set off several weeks ago for a warmer land. The swallow had stayed behind because he had fallen in love with a slender reed by the river, and he could not bear to leave her. But the wind had grown chill and the bite of frost had crept into the air. The shivering swallow had realised that to stay any longer would mean certain death from the cold. He had begged the reed to travel with him, but the reed had

simply shaken her
head. So the swallow
had been forced to fly sadly
off without her. Tomorrow he
would fly away and catch up with his
friends. Now the little bird tucked his head
under his wing and prepared to get some rest for the
long journey. But just as the swallow began to drift off into dreams,
large raindrops started to fall on his head. The swallow looked up in
puzzlement at the clear night sky and saw that the statue above him
was crying.

"Who are you and why are you weeping?" the little swallow
asked, as the statue's tears shone in the moonlight like diamonds.

"People call me the Happy Prince," replied the statue, "but in
truth, I am full of sadness. They have set me up here so high that I
can look out over the whole city and see all its ugliness and misery.
Tonight, I can see a poor woman sitting in a house near the edge of
town. The woman is thin from hunger and pale from tiredness, but
she is still at work, sewing passion-flowers onto a gown for one of
the queen's maids-of-honour. In the corner of the room, her little boy
lies very ill in bed, asking for oranges. But the woman has no money

to buy him anything, so all she can give him is water." The Happy Prince sighed. "Little swallow, will you pluck out the ruby from my sword and take it to the woman, so that she might sell it to the jeweller for money? My feet are fastened to this pedestal and I cannot move."

The Happy Prince looked so sad that the swallow agreed to be his messenger. The little bird pecked the ruby out of the prince's sword and flew away with it in his beak over the rooftops. He flew in at the window of the woman's house and found her slumped over her work in a worn-out sleep. The swallow laid the jewel down next to her thimble, then he flew gently round the bed, fanning the feverish, sick boy with his wings until he looked much cooler and more comfortable. Then the swallow flew back to the Happy Prince and told him what he had done. "It's strange," the bird remarked. "I feel a warm glow inside me, even though the weather is so cold."

"That is because you have done a good deed," explained the Happy Prince, as the tired little swallow closed his eyes.

Next day, the swallow flew all over the city bidding goodbye to everyone and everything. "I am leaving tonight for Egypt!" he cried. But when in the evening he came to say farewell to the Happy Prince, he found that the statue was crying once again.

"Far across the city I can see into an attic where a young man leans over a desk. He is struggling to finish a play for the Director of the Theatre, but he is too cold to write anymore. His fire has died away and he has no money to buy either wood or any food for his supper." A glistening tear rolled off the end of the Happy Prince's nose and sploshed onto the swallow's head. "Little swallow, will you stay with me one more night and be my messenger? Will you pluck out one of my sapphire eyes and take it to him?"

"Dear prince," said the swallow, "I will not pluck out your eye." and tears gleamed in his own.

"Little swallow, please do as I ask," begged the Happy Prince, and he looked so sad that the swallow fluttered up and plucked out one of his sapphire eyes and flew away with it to the young man in the attic. The little swallow was very relieved when he returned to nestle at the Happy Prince's feet, for the air underneath his wings had really become very cold indeed.

The next day, the swallow flew down to the harbour and watched all the big ships sailing away to lands where the breezes were warm and the days were long. "I am leaving too, tonight!" he sang out to everyone he saw. At sunset, the swallow flew off to the Happy Prince to say goodbye. "In the square below," said the Happy Prince, "I can see a little matchgirl whose matches have all spilled into the gutter. She is crying because she can make no money and if she goes home empty-handed, her father will beat her." The Happy Prince smiled sadly. "Little swallow, pluck out my other eye and take it to the little matchgirl so she can be happy."

"But then you will be blind!" cried the swallow.

"Little swallow, please do as I ask," whispered the Happy Prince, and he looked so sad that the bird did as he wanted.

"Now you can no longer see," the little swallow said, as he fluttered back to the statue. "I will stay with you always."

"But little swallow," protested the Happy Prince, "your friends will be waiting for you on the hazy banks of the River Nile."

"I will stay with you always and be your eyes," the swallow promised, and he slept between the prince's feet.

Next day, the swallow flew all over the city and told the Happy Prince what he had seen there. "I have seen the rich making merry in their beautiful houses while beggars lie outside their gates," the swallow murmured. "I have seen old people who sit all day on their own, cold and lonely. I have seen small children tremble in front of bullies. I have seen much suffering and misery."

"Little swallow," said the prince, "with your beak, peel off the fine gold that covers me. Fly with leaves of it to all the poor people of my city."

The little swallow sighed heavily, but he did what he was told. Then the statue of the Happy Prince was quite dull and grey.

As the faithful bird finally settled down between his friend's feet, the snow began to fall in thick white flakes. The streets glistened silver with a lining of frost. Icicles hung like shards of glass from the rooftops. And the little swallow shivered at the foot of the Happy Prince. He tried beating his wings to keep warm, but eventually he knew that he was going to die. The little swallow used his last drop of strength to flutter up to the prince's shoulder. "Goodbye, Happy Prince," he cried. "I will not see you again."

"I am glad you are finally going to where the sun will warm your wings," the Happy Prince said.

"I am not going to Egypt," murmured the swallow, "I am going to sleep forever." And he kissed the Happy Prince on the lips and fell down dead at his feet.

That very moment, a strange cracking noise came from within the Happy Prince. It was so loud that the Mayor heard it way down below. He peered up at the statue for the first time in months. "Good lord!" he remarked. "However did the Happy Prince get that shabby? We'll have to replace him with something else."

The very next day, workmen pulled down the Happy Prince from his column and threw him into a furnace. They cleared away the dead swallow and then put a statue of the Mayor on the column instead. But the Happy Prince knew nothing about all this, because his heart had broken. In fact, when the workmen opened the door of the furnace, they saw his cracked lead heart for themselves, because it would not melt away. They threw it onto the same rubbish dump on which they had thrown the dead swallow was lying. And when God asked his angels to bring him the two most precious things in all the city, they took the Happy Prince's heart and the little swallow with them up to heaven.